BROKEN

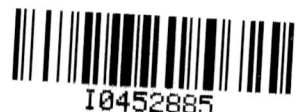

ALSO BY LONNI LEES

Crawlspace
Deranged
The Mosaic Murder
The Corpse in the Cactus

BROKEN

LONNI LEES

WILDSIDE PRESS

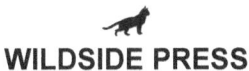

Published by Wildside Press LLC.
wildsidepress.com

PROLOGUE

The clacking noise of brittle bone against brittle bone was swallowed by the hot desert air leaving only silence. The hard, dry earth of Camino Del Diablo kept its secrets well and held tightly to the hand jutting up from the cracked desert floor. Crooked fingers reached upward, long picked clean by vultures. Scavengers and blowing desert sand had blasted and picked away at the bright red nail polish on the hand that had once reached for the stars. Now it pointed toward the Tule Mountains of Arizona. Like a road sign from hell, one crippled finger pointed toward the Mexican border, another toward the wildlife refuge of Cabeza Prieta.

Only the foolish or desperate dared challenge this unforgiving terrain.

In the distance a car kicked up dust then slowed to a stop along the shoulder of the unpaved road. A man and woman got out. The man was handsome with the dark and sun toughened skin of someone who'd spent his life working outdoors. He threw his head back, drained the last drops of tequila from the bottle, then hurled it high into the air. The woman laughed and lifted her skirt. "Come and get it, Cal," she teased.

"You're a naughty girl, Kandi," he said, walking towards her.

Lifting her skirt higher she exposed more than her bare legs. "That's what you love about me," she giggled. "Come to mama."

Cal didn't need any encouragement.

This deserted stretch of nowhere had proven to be the perfect spot for their illicit trysts.

He lifted her up and sat her on the car's hood.

"Jesus Christ Cal, I know you want me hot, but I didn't know you wanted me toasted. This metal is as hot as a griddle!"

Kandi reached forward, grabbed his shoulders and bounced against Cal, wrapped her tanned and naked legs around his waist and slowly wiggled downward towards the prize that jutted from his unzipped pants. That was his best asset. He was always willing, hard and ready, unlike the old but wealthy geezer she'd married. With Cal she had the best of both worlds.

Grunts and giggles danced across the desert floor and kissed the shallow grave.

I'm here. I'm over here. I'm trying to wave, but my hand won't move.

Why am I here? Can you give me a ride? I want to go home. I'm lonely and I'm lost. Look, over here. See me, please see me.

Sweating body slid against sweating body as they played their familiar sexual symphony. Three more aggressive thrusts and they were finished. Cal zipped his pants as Kandi pulled down her skirt. They got into the car, catching their breath from the heat of their pleasure and the thick desert air.

"When are you going to tell him?" he asked, looking at her perfect silhouette as she stared out the dusty windshield.

"I told you already. When the time is right."

"I've heard that a hundred times. I love you Kandi. I want us to be together, no more hiding and sneaking around. Just you and me. When are you going to dump him so we can move on with our lives?"

"Our time will come," she said.

I'm here. I'm right over here. Can't you hear me?

"Soon honey, I promise. I'm just waiting for the right moment. Be patient."

Cal leaned over and put his arm around her. "How about just one more go-round before we head back?" Sometimes Cal felt as if their sex was the only thing that truly got her attention. He wanted more than that. He wanted all of her, not just these hidden, stolen moments.

"There's no time. Not today. The hubby's flying in from his business trip and if he decides to take an earlier flight we're both fucked."

"Do you have any idea what it feels like? Me, cleaning his pool, tending the grounds, while you lie upstairs in that ridiculous mansion, his bloated body on top of you, grunting as he tries to get the job done with his limp, worthless dick? Why do you do it Kandi? Why?"

She didn't answer.

She didn't have to.

"And mowing all that lawn. What kind of rich, pompous idiot grows a lawn in the middle of the desert anyway? His water bill from that sprinkler system alone is more than I earn from a month of hard labor."

Kandi laughed. "Are you jealous because he has money?"

"No, because he has you."

Help me. Can't you hear me calling?

They didn't hear her. No one ever did.

Find me.

Take me home.

Were her eyes nothing but empty sockets filled with sand there would have been tears.

Tears for herself. There was no one else to cry for her. There was no one who knew she was gone, or even cared.

Her killer had chosen her resting place wisely, then carelessly tossed her body into the hole he'd dug. No prayers were said over her as he covered her with a blanket of sand.

Her pile of bones shared the vast graveyard with others. They were the flotsam and jetsam of broken souls and broken bones, floating eternally on this waterless sea. They were miners from the 1800's gold rush. Some had died of thirst, others by a greedy hand on a hot trigger, relieving them of what little treasure they had found. They were crossers from Mexico, the women, the children, the desperate who perished in their quest for a better life. And then there were victims not unlike herself.

But for the occasional wildflower that would sprout reverently above an unmarked grave, they were forgotten.

ONE

It was a town where washed up cops came to die. The lousy paycheck was better than becoming a mall cop or a comatose night watchman. They could still hold a gun and work at what they loved. If they'd been removed from other departments for being too quick on the trigger, or being on the take, or being psychologically unstable, it didn't matter here. The town was happy to have some legal hired guns on the cheap, no questions asked.

Big Jim Bullock was an exception, as was fellow cop and best friend Trick Delgado.

Trick was born and raised in Agua Verde. He'd seen other places, places he'd rather forget, some beautiful and some ugly wastelands, but he'd left his adventures behind him and returned. Agua Verde was home. And home was where he wanted to be.

Jim slowly edged his squad car around the corner and onto a dimly lit side street. The weekends were generally quiet in Agua Verde, Arizona. Week nights like this were deader yet. That suited him just fine. He preferred the leisurely pace here to Phoenix or even Tucson. Fewer people meant fewer murders, fewer gangs, less graffiti. And a lot less work. With a population of a mere 35,000 the town had just enough big city amenities to be comfortable, while being spared a lot of the big city problems.

Jim didn't like problems.

Unlike some cops, Big Jim didn't get off on the adrenaline rush that comes with confrontation. He'd rather use wit and words than bullets to quell the occasional domestic dispute or petty crime.

Less hassle, less paperwork.

Firing his gun was a last resort.

Despite his laid-back demeanor, he managed to maintain a tough-guy reputation in the department and was looked up to by his fellow officers. They knew that when push came to shove Big Jim Bullock had their backs. Jim was cop to the bone. He lived, breathed and probably bled the same shade of blue as the faded uniforms they wore.

But he'd be the first to pull the trigger if the situation truly called for it.

He'd un-holstered it a few times, but he'd never once had to fire his gun in the line of duty.

Not that the occasional gun battle didn't take place in Agua Verde. People were people everywhere. The good, the bad and the in-between. When tempers flared, Jim's imposing and muscular six-foot-two frame, and a few well-chosen words, usually diffused a situation before it got out of control crazy.

The other officers respected him and he respected himself.

Jim turned the next corner onto a street dappled with strip malls and garish neon. Dimly lit street lamps cast minimal light onto the discount stores, bodegas and bars. The neon lights of Flaming June's buzzed and sputtered. June's was the local haven for society's misfits. The gay and lesbian community that congregated there also welcomed the goths, the tattooed and tattered, the shaved heads or purple streaked hair, the beautiful or ugly, the straight or crooked. Her arms opened wide in welcome to the outcasts and rebels that lived on the outer edges, giving them a non-judgmental place to call home.

Surprisingly, they were rarely the town's trouble makers.

They just wanted to be left alone to live life on their own terms.

Flaming June's was the one place in Agua Verde where they could drink in relative peace. The only time the law got involved was when a patron drank to the point of stupid and flexed his drunk muscles. Bar fights were bar fights, be they at Flaming June's, the local biker bar or the private golf resort at the edge of town.

Nothing made a man stupid faster than a gut full of booze. Happy drunks, ornery drunks, mean drunks. Big Jim had seen them all, but for those who silently drank themselves into a stupor, he'd provide a safe ride home.

Agua Verde's lone presiding judge, the Honorable Gareth Lambert, had been his passenger more times than he cared to count.

The first drops of soft monsoon rain gently washed the desert grit from the street and sidewalks. Dark and wet, it splattered and nudged the neon reflections across the pavement, leaving a gash of crimson in its wake. It trickled like blood across the cracks and over the curb, until it was swallowed by the thirsty gutters.

A *Mariachi* tune floated through the night from Jalisco's Cantina across the way. The notes danced across the street then collided with the pure tones from Benny Goodman's clarinet be-bopping its way from inside Flaming June's as her front door opened. The two songs blended, creating a cacophonous melody that filled the night air.

A lone figure exited the bar and cautiously made its way up the sidewalk. His diminutive frame suggested he was little more than a child and Jim wondered if the kid had been carded when he entered the bar or if they'd just looked the other way. When the kid reached the corner a group of thugs emerged from the shadows and pounced on him. He fell to the pavement with the first blow. They proceeded to hit and kick him, one after the other, then all at once. They laughed and yelped like hungry hyenas as they stomped and kicked the cowering, helpless figure. Their war-whoops and the man's girlish screams punctuated the music that filled the air.

"Faggot!" One of them yelled as he kicked him in the ribs.

"Stinking butt-sniffer," taunted another.

The young man covered his face as he curled into a protective fetal position.

Another hard blow to the stomach and he stopped screaming.

But the laughter and the beating continued.

Big Jim Bullock rolled down his squad car window and flashed a bright light on them. Like sewer rats, the hooded shadows scurried and disappeared into the black crevasses of the night. Jim radioed for back up and an ambulance, exited the car, un-holstered his gun and raced down the sidewalk to where the young man lay.

His motionless body was as bloody as a slaughterhouse floor.

Jim holstered his gun, then knelt down and felt the boy's neck for a pulse. It was weak. It was more important to stay with him than try to chase down his assailants. When they arrived, back-up could go look for the chicken-shit bastards. They were likely street-gang wannabee's or teenagers who got their kicks preying on the weak and helpless. It was sport for them. A game. They found joy in inflicting pain. It was a sickness for which there was no cure. Short of a bullet. These blights on civilized society were one of the few things that could tempt Big Jim Bullock to pull the trigger with no regrets.

There had been a few gay bashings in Agua Verde, as well as assaults on the homeless. No one had been caught. One of the street people had been beaten into permanent brain damage. And a permanent home, where he'd spend the rest of his life being fed through tubes in a charity hospital bed.

The thugs continued to strike, then disappeared like phantoms.

He'd like to get a hold of them.

One at a time.

Jim held the kid's delicate hand. He looked like a wounded bird. A little sparrow.

Sirens howled in the distance.

The boy's lids fluttered, then his dark eyes opened, looking directly into Jim's. There was a faint smile on his bruised and bloodied mouth.

"¿Es usted un ángel?" He whispered.

Jim's grasp of Spanish was spotty at best, but he got the gist of it.

"No, I'm no angel," he answered. "I'm a cop."

"Creo que tú eres mi ángel."

"Do you speak English?" Jim asked. "Uh, do you *habla* the English?"

"*Si, poquito.*" His lids closed. "I think you are my angel," he said, then passed out.

Tires and brakes squealed as the ambulance and two squad cars pulled up.

"Over here," Jim motioned to the ambulance attendants. "I need help. Now!"

Two officers ran over to Jim as the boy was lifted onto the stretcher and carried to the ambulance.

"Holy Jesus," said Trick Delgado, looking at the pool of blood on the sidewalk. Trick was a broad-shouldered, balding, five foot ten, with a south of the border complexion contrasted by piercing Irish gray eyes. An Agua Verde native, he'd entered the local police force as soon as he'd had enough of his other life. If you make a wrong turn the best you can do is slam on the brakes and head back in the right direction. He wanted to help the helpless, so becoming a cop had been his ambition for as far back as he could remember and he regretted having been sidetracked along the way. Oh, he'd been praised, even awarded for his stellar service to his country, but it was nothing more than a bad dream that faded, then disappeared. That was then, but this was now.

"This looks really bad," Trick said to his friend. "What the fuck happened?"

"Another gay bashing outside Flaming June's. I counted five of them. Just shadows in hoodies. That's all I could see. You guys drive around and see what you can find."

"Just one more queer," said the cop named Mackey Hogan, exhaling an audible snort through his pudgy, whiskey-veined nose.

"He's a victim, you son-of-a bitch. Get the lead out, now!" Jim said as he headed for the ambulance. "I'm following to the hospital."

"Let's go," said Trick Delgado to Mackey. "You head towards Main and I'll go to the south. With a little luck, they might still be on the streets."

He shrugged and leisurely followed Trick.

"You can really be an ass-hole," Trick said to Mackey.

"What's the matter, Trick? You a fairy lover?" Mackey asked, throwing him a noisy kiss as he walked towards his car.

They got into their dark blue cars and took off in opposite directions.

Two attendants shoved the stretcher into the back of the ambulance. The door slammed shut with a loud bang.

"How's it look?" Jim asked.

"Not good. Not good at all," said the driver. "The guy's really messed up."

"Then step on it!"

Big Jim Bullock ran to his car, slid behind the wheel and followed the flashing red lights through the dark streets as it raced to Our Lady of Guadalupe hospital. He paced the dark hospital hallways until three in the morning before a doctor finally appeared.

"It was touch and go," the doctor told him. "Two broken ribs, a broken leg, multiple lacerations. And he's got a pretty bad concussion."

"Cut to the chase, doc. Is he going to be okay?"

"We were finally able to stop the internal bleeding. Bottom line, it looks like he's going to make it."

"I need to speak with him."

"He's pretty doped up," said the doctor. "So keep it short." He led Jim to the recovery room.

"Five minutes," he said.

When the doctor left, Jim pulled up a chair and sat down. He reached over and took the young man's hand.

"How 'ya feeling, kid?"

Slowly the boy opened his eyes, blinked, and looked at the officer.

"I am no kid, *senõr.* I am twenty-three," he said with pride. "All grown up."

"I need your name."

"Mi nombre?"

"For the report."

"Paco," he whispered as he tried to focus on Jim's face. He broke into a pained grin. "Oh, it is you, *amigo.* You are the man who is my angel."

That suited Jim just fine. He'd been called a lot of names on the job, but angel definitely wasn't one of them.

TWO

Paco lay in the hospital bed for two weeks and the cop he saw as his savior visited him daily. He had no idea who had attacked him nor did the police. It was looking like another dead end. One more gay bashing to add to the previous attacks on the homosexuals and the homeless of Agua Verde.

It appeared that Big Jim Bullock was the only person who cared if the young man in the hospital bed lived or died. Just a cop named Jim. And maybe the doctor, but that was his job. Jim was Paco's only visitor and with each visit he came to know the victim more. Paco was a gentle soul and there was a sadness about him that tugged at Jim's heart.

"You're looking better all the time," he said. "The bruises are almost gone."

"They say it is a miracle I am alive," said Paco.

"And there's better news. The doc says you're ready to go home as long as there's someone to look after you," said Jim. "There's going to be more rehabilitation and you'll need help. That leg is still healing."

"There is no one."

"You must have some family who can look after you. A mother? A sister? A father?"

"No more. No, there is no one," he said. "To *mi familia,* I am *muerte.* I am dead, Mister Chim."

"I don't understand." Jim smiled at Paco's pronunciation of his name.

"*Macho,* that is *muy* important in our culture. Very important. I am not so much that," he laughed. "I am not manly," he said with a flip of his wrist. "My father, he was—what is the word? Horrified. Yes, he was horrified when he discovered I was less than a man. That I was *afeminado.* Gay. He disowned me, told me that to the family I was now dead. I was kicked out. Of the *casa* and the family. They want nothing to do with me."

"I could contact them. I can't believe they wouldn't want to help you."

"No. It would do no good. In their eyes I am dead. I am no longer."

All that Jim could think of to say was, "I'm sorry."

"You are the one who saved me. You are my angel. Do not be sorry, Chim. It is not your fault."

"It's wrong," said Jim, as much to himself as to Paco. "The one thing we have, when everything else in the world goes wrong, is the support of family. At least that's the way it's supposed to be."

A nurse entered the room and ushered Jim out so she could go about her business. He paced the hallway, thinking. Until he'd rescued Paco, he'd always distanced himself from those with whom he came in contact. The only time the guilty saw him after an arrest was when he appeared in court to testify against them. After that he was done. It wasn't because he didn't care, but keeping his distance from the perpetrators, and especially from the victims, made the job easier.

If a cop let himself get too close it was overwhelming. You spent your days seeing the worst in people. Trying to clean up the damage. Facing the senseless violence and the tragedy it brought to innocent lives. You were seen as a uniform, with all the connotations that uniform represented, everything from enemy to peacekeeper. More often than not you were looked upon as the adversary rather than the protector. It could get to you and you had to learn to let it go.

You had to leave it behind you at the end of your shift. It wasn't easy, but if you weren't careful you'd be swallowed by the darkness until you were no longer able to see the light.

He'd seen it happen. He'd seen the depression grab hold of a cop so tight that he couldn't climb out of the black hole.

He'd seen it ruin their marriages, haunt their nightmares, ruin their perspective, ruin their lives until nothing was left but the darkness.

Big Jim Bullock had no intention of being one more cop who ate his gun.

A tap on his shoulder made him jump.

"You can go back in now," the nurse said. "But keep it short. Visiting hours are almost over."

The backwards glance she gave him as she entered the next room didn't escape him. It was as if she were trying to size him up. Hell, he was working on that himself, he thought with a shrug as he reentered Paco's room.

"That nurse, she is *la monstra.* A monster. She comes just to poke me with her needles."

"The worst of it's behind you," Jim reassured him.

The mysterious bedside machines droned and beeped, accentuating the awkward silence.

Finally Paco spoke.

"Sometimes I don't understand," he said. "My older brother, he is in a gang. He has been in jail for doing bad things. But he is still welcome in the family. I have never caused trouble but they threw me away. You say I still need to be looked after but there is no one."

Paco looked around the room.

“Do you think they will let me stay here?” He asked. “It’s okay except for the horrible food. It is as white and bland as the *gringos* who are afraid of good spices.”

Jim took Paco’s hand and leaned forward, looking into his dark, sad eyes.

“I could take you home with me,” he finally said.

And he did.

THREE

The desert sun crept over the horizon like a cat stalking its prey. It erased the morning shadows from the side of the turquoise adobe house as faint slivers of steam rose from the ground, erasing the last vestiges of last nights welcome rain from the thirst-quenched landscape, brushing quickly across it until all that remained was the familiar cracked, dry earth.

Shards of light shone through the streaked window and washed across the kitchen table. Ingrid Delgado stood over her husband Trick and topped off his cup of morning coffee. Wearing a simple pale gray two-piece suit with a white blouse, she was dressed for work. Her summer-white high-heeled shoes clicked across the terra cotta tiled floor as she returned the coffee pot to its place on the burner, then clicked again as she returned to the table and sat in the chair across from him.

"It's going to be another long day," she said, running her long fingernails through her shoulder-length natural blonde hair.

"Isn't it always?"

"Some days are longer than others. I have to go to the hospital," she said. "The little boy they brought in last night is critical."

"I heard about it. Mackey Hogan had him brought in. He said the kid couldn't have been more than three or four, but it was hard to tell as thin as he was. He said the apartment was a disaster zone. Dirty dishes everywhere. Piles of trash heaped half way to the ceiling. The stench was overwhelming enough to make him gag. And Mackey's no softy. He said the place was crawling with bugs so bad that the carpet looked like it was moving beneath his feet."

"How can people live like that?" Her genetically ingrained obsession with orderliness and cleanliness shuddered at the image.

"A neighbor had called it in, said she couldn't stand the noise any more, that the cockroaches were invading her own apartment. She said she'd never seen a kid, but knew there was one because she was sick and tired of hearing his cries and screams. She yelled into the phone that sometimes he was so loud she couldn't hear her own television."

"And that's why she called? Because she couldn't hear the damn tv?"

"Go figure. Anyway, Mackey answered the call and drove out there.

When she finally opened the door for him, it was evident the mother was high on something and the boy was neglected. He said the pitiful, naked kid just looked up at him from where he sat on the floor covered in his own feces. He had a blank look, as if there was nothing behind his eyes or in front of them."

"Neglected? That's an understatement. He was emaciated and full of cigarette burns. He wasn't neglected Trick, he was tortured."

Trick winced.

Ingrid was a child psychiatrist with the county. He wondered how she faced her job every day. She dealt with things equally as bad as he did, or even worse. He locked up the crooks and she tried to heal the victims. There were days when they both felt defeated. Ingrid was strong and she was tough, it was the German in her, but even so there were days that he could tell broke her heart. She maintained a professional exterior, but it ate at her, he could tell. Try as she might, she couldn't hide it.

Not from him anyway.

That sensitive side was one of the reasons he loved her, even if she did try to keep it hidden. She was good at her job because she cared.

The toast popped up from the toaster causing Ingrid to jump, nearly spilling her coffee.

"Are you okay?" Trick asked.

"Fine. I'm just fine, Trick. I'm a little jumpy today, that's all."

"Want to share?"

"Not really."

He shrugged.

"You know what's the worst of it?" She asked, slamming her coffee mug down, spilling some on the table. She rose, unrolled some paper towels and returned to the table. As she sopped up the spilled coffee, she resumed speaking. "I'll tell you exactly what's the worst of it. It's the system. It's the damn rules we have to follow. Why is our goal to reunite the family? For what reason? It's bullshit, Trick. They give the parents counseling, then send the kids back for more abuse. They should never have to go back. That child, any child, is more important than preserving some dysfunctional family unit. They need to be rescued, not sent back to the wolves."

"If I ran the world," mumbled Trick. "It's for damn sure that the people in the midst of things have a better grasp of the realities than the ones making the rules."

Ingrid rose from her chair and walked over to the counter where she fished out the toast, quickly tossing the dark tan slices onto two small plates as they burned her fingers.

Trick pushed his chair back, stood, and walked over to the refrigerator.

He opened the door and removed a stick of butter and some orange marmalade, then sat them on the counter next to Ingrid.

"I remember that one little girl. What was her name? Emily something?" he asked, as he removed two butter knives from the drawer and handed one to his wife.

"Yes, her name was Emily. I rest my case. Not two weeks after she was returned to her mother," Ingrid choked on the words, "she was raped and strangled to death by the new boyfriend. She was just a little girl, Trick."

She slathered some butter and marmalade onto her toast.

"And the mother tried to defend the son-of-a-bitch. I remember that." He said, "It was like the kid was disposable."

"She was convicted as an accessory, but that didn't bring back little Emily, did it?"

Trick draped his arm around her shoulder. Her reaction was subtle, but he felt her recoil from his touch.

"Are you sure you're going to be alright?" he asked.

"I'm fine, Trick," she said, raising her voice. "Everything's just rosy."

She grabbed her plate of toast and returned to the table. Trick followed and sat down across from her.

"I'm sorry, Trick. I didn't mean to snap at you. I'm a little edgy today, that's all."

He bit into his toast, looking at her as if trying to solve a Chinese puzzle box. Something wasn't right, something more than the boy in the hospital, but he knew better than to push. Some days she was warm as a winter blanket, but other times she was a block of polar ice and nothing could melt her. Experience had taught him that she'd talk when she was good and ready.

They ate their toast in silence, then drained the last drops of coffee from their mugs.

Ingrid looked over at him and smiled.

"When you see Jim Bullock invite him over for Saturday dinner."

"Okay, what are you up to now?"

"I've got a new friend I'd like him to meet."

"Ingrid, Ingrid," he sighed. "Not one of your fix-ups panned out, you know that."

"I think this one might be different."

"You're spinning your wheels."

"We'll find the right woman for him yet. He's a good catch, Trick."

"And a damn hard one."

"Just invite him, okay? What's the worst that could happen? A good meal and good company. I like Jim as much as you do and we don't get together often enough. We need more in our lives than our jobs."

Ingrid rose and placed her coffee mug and plate in the sink.

"Are you sure you're going to be alright?" he asked.

"Would you stop asking me that?" She squared her shoulders. "I'm always alright. Things just get to me sometimes, that's all."

"You've made a difference. Have you forgotten the Morales kids? You saved those boys. And the foster parents fought right along with you."

"And they hit the same brick walls."

"It was your testimony that finally saved them."

"The older boy was damn near comatose by then. The mother had supervised visitation and it wasn't until she hurled the boy across the room that anyone listened."

"But you won. And you'll win again."

Ingrid shrugged.

"You deserve a lot of credit," Trick said. "Don't short-change yourself."

"Happy endings are for fairytales."

She picked up her purse and keys from the counter, hesitated, then leaned over and gave him an obligatory kiss on the top of his balding head.

"I'll see you tonight," she said, tossed her purse across her shoulder and walked out the door.

FOUR

Big Jim Bullock walked into the guest bedroom and opened the blinds. The morning sun filled the room like a floodlight, waking Paco. The large mattress made him appear even smaller than he was, like the last abandoned fledgling in the nest. He blinked his eyes and looked up at the man standing over him. Pulling the comforter over his face, he held it above his nose, so that only his dark eyes peered out.

He giggled like a little girl.

"What's so funny, sport?"

"I thought I was dreaming, but it is real," he said, lowering the comforter to expose a wide grin. "I wake up in a beautiful mansion with my angel standing over me."

Two bedrooms in a subdivision is hardly a mansion, Jim thought. Granted, it was a step up from Paco's hospital room, and God only knew where he'd been before that. Wandering the streets? Sleeping in alleys? Or something even worse.

He didn't want to know. A person does whatever he has to do to survive.

The bedroom filled with the aroma of frying bacon and fresh coffee from the kitchen.

"I started breakfast," Jim said.

"*Gracias!* I am hungry like a javelina."

"Good. Now get up before it's burned or cold."

"You will help me, *señor* Chim?" Paco asked, reaching out his arms.

"Nope. You've got to learn to get around on that cast all by yourself. I'm not going to be here twenty-four-seven to wait on you."

"You are mean, like the nurse who poked me with needles," he pouted.

Paco used his elbows to push himself up, then swung his injured leg out the side of the bed. The heavy cast thumped against the floor. He pushed himself up and swung out the other leg, puffing at the effort. He sat there, scowling up at Jim, then crossed his arms and flopped backwards onto the bed.

"I go back to bed now," he said.

"No, you get up now. By yourself. This isn't some fancy hotel and I'm not serving you breakfast in bed. If you want to eat, I'll see you in the kitchen. If not, you can go hungry."

Paco whined.

Big Jim Bullock walked out of the room, leaving Paco to either struggle and succeed or give up. It was Paco's choice and Jim wasn't going to waste time arguing with him. Besides, it would be too damn easy for him to give in and spoil him rotten. He deserved some kindness, but what he needed most was to build some strength, both physically and emotionally. Paco was an innocent and downright endearing, but Big Jim Bullock wasn't going to fold under the whimpers and protests. The kid needed to toughen up.

"I can always send you back to Nurse Ratchet!" He bellowed as he headed toward the kitchen.

Jim was fishing bacon strips from their sea of grease when he heard a small voice behind him. "*Buenos dias, senõr* Chim. I did not mean to speak bad to you." Jim turned around to face a pouting Paco who stood leaning against the doorway. He was wearing one of Jim's tee shirts. It hung to his knees just above the cast on his leg.

"I knew you could do it."

"Only because I am *mucho* hungry."

"Whatever works. How many eggs do you want?" he asked, reaching for the carton.

"*Dos, por favor.* No, three. Three *huevos* would be very nice."

Jim motioned for him to sit at the table. Paco took one step, then huffed and puffed his way across the room, sighing loudly as he plopped into the chair.

"It won't work," Jim said.

"What?"

"Your drama."

Jim could feel Paco's pout as he turned away from him. He flipped over the eggs, then lifted them out of the pan and onto the plates. He sat them on the table. Paco took a bite of the eggs, wrinkled his nose, then looked up at Jim.

"Do you have hot sauce? I taste no flavor."

"I'll pick up some on my way home. Anything else for your highness?" The sarcasm had obviously escaped him.

"Chorizo."

"Cho-what?"

"It is very good. I will show you the proper way how to cook *huevos*."

"Your gratitude overwhelms me."

"*Gracias,* Chim," he grinned. "But I will be alone all day?"

Before Jim could answer, Paco laid into his breakfast as if he hadn't eaten in weeks. He was beginning to suspect that the kid, not unlike the sparrow he resembled, could eat his weight in food.

"I've got a job. If you get hungry there's food in the fridge and bread on the counter. Help yourself." Jim was beginning to feel as if he'd brought the wrong dog home from the pound.

"I am so grateful to you," Paco said. "You are *mucho* good to me."

Then Paco looked over at him with his deep brown cocker spaniel eyes.

Paco pointed at his cast and asked, "How do I shower and not get this wet? The doctor said not to get it wet."

"You can't."

"Oh!" he said, fluttering his eyelashes, "I am going to stink like a skunk."

"Use the bathtub and hang your leg over the side to keep it dry."

Paco looked baffled, like he'd just been asked to solve the mystery of the universe.

"I'll help you when I get home. Any more questions?" Jim's rescue was starting to remind him of an annoying kid who keeps asking "why?" over and over again.

"Only one more, I promise," he said, sensing the man's growing impatience.

"Go on."

"What am I to do here *all alone?"* He asked in a final ploy for sympathy.

It didn't work.

Jim rose, motioning him to follow.

Slowly and silently, Paco followed him into the living room and sat in a recliner as Jim ordered, pulling the lever to elevate his broken leg. Jim handed him the tv remote.

"Watch tv. Or take a movie from the cabinet over there. There's music. There are books," he said, pointing to the wall of bookshelves.

"I do not read so very well," he said, lowering his eyes.

"Then look at the damn pictures," Jim said. "There's art books third shelf down."

"*Gracias, senõr* Chim!" Paco yelled as Jim walked out the door.

Big Jim Bullock inhaled a deep breath of hot morning air as he closed the door behind him. What have I gotten myself into? he thought as he headed for his car.

FIVE

One thing Trick Delgado hated was trouble. And he was sensing trouble on the horizon with Ingrid and it pissed him off that he couldn't figure out the what or why of it.

It's going to be another hot one, he thought as he pulled his car into the parking lot of Wong's corner store. It was a run-down little place, its dusty shelves filled with mysterious Asian inventory and overpriced groceries, but Jia Wong always had an urn of good coffee brewing. And he needed a decent one before he faced the day. Trick didn't have the heart to tell Ingrid her coffee was sludge. Or that it was worse than the crap at the police station. As much as he loved his caffeine, it wasn't that important. Why make waves over something as trivial as a cup of joe? If he'd picked one room for Ingrid to be good in, it wouldn't have been the kitchen. A warm bed trumped a good meal any day. He'd hit the jackpot with wife number four and he wasn't going to screw it up.

Wife number one had been a mistake from the get-go, he'd be the first to admit it. He'd first met her when he booked her for prostitution and in his youthful optimism thought he could save her. Before they'd crossed paths her longest relationships had been one night stands. He was dumb enough to think love could heal anything. And she had the palest blue eyes he'd ever seen. Eyes that lured him in and wouldn't let go. He'd always been a sucker for a pretty face. But not even a wedding ring did the trick for that one. There was an emptiness deep within her that nothing could fill and eventually she'd walked away and back to her comfort zone on the streets. Old habits were hard to break and they were so deeply ingrained in her that she couldn't let them go. It could have been worse. They could have had kids.

Their paths still crossed from time to time, usually in the booking room. Any love or pity he'd felt for her had died long ago. What had once been a cute little honey now wore the mask of an ageing crack whore, complete with rotting teeth and a body upholstered in flesh that never stopped itching. She found an inexplicable satisfaction in dancing with her demons that was beyond his understanding. He doubted she even recognized him and he wouldn't have known it was her but for those bright blue eyes, now bloodshot and unfocused. She was nothing but a reminder of his failed role as savior.

Live and learn.

Wife number two was way too young and not ready to settle down. She'd proven that when he'd come home early and found her in bed with fellow officer Mackey Hogan. He could have shot Mackey. Hell, he could have shot the wife and made a dead meat sandwich from the two of them.

But neither was worth it.

Mackey had taunted him, saying her best asset was she could suck a golf ball through a garden hose. And when Mackey told him if you marry a whore you get a whore for a wife, those were the truest words the bastard had ever uttered. Even if they were worthy of a bullet hole between his eyes.

It was easier to just sign the divorce papers and be done with it.

Trick saw Agua Verde as an island, lost in a sea of desert rather than an ocean, but just as isolated. It was a small town with an even smaller police force and things ran smoother if everybody got along. It made enclosed spaces more palatable.

So he worked at it.

Mackey at least had the courtesy to dump the cheating bitch and move on to the next trophy on his list.

Mackey Hogan never could keep his mouth shut or his dick in his pants.

As for wife number three, Rosey was a hot little number with flaming red hair and a temper to match. Ingrid had suggested that he'd been looking for someone like his mother. Those damn shamrock earrings she always wore should've given him a clue. They screamed Irish, never the favorite side of his own lineage. There was never a dull moment with that one, but a little peace and quiet now and then would have been nice. He was relieved when things went down the dumper and never put much thought into the reason.

One day she'd been there and the next day she was gone, most likely back to her family in South Boston where hot tempers and foul mouths were the normal means of communication. He never tried to track her down. He'd had enough of her and the last thing he wanted was an encore to her never ending drama. After awhile he filed for divorce on the grounds of desertion and moved on. The Southies were welcome to her.

Then he met Ingrid. She had an icy exterior that hid a warm heart. She was successful and grounded. She was a lady. Because of their work they shared common ground.

And she didn't have a rap sheet.

He'd finally found a keeper.

Trick Delgado smiled as he exited the car, walked across the hot pavement and into Wong's.

Jia Wong's diminutive frame was hunched over the counter reading a newspaper written in strange Chinese symbols. She looked up at him as he walked through the door and into the store.

"Coffee fresh and hot," she said to him. "Tea be better, but no one want tea. Only coffee."

"I guess it's a cultural thing," he said, then wondered if he'd sounded politically incorrect. "Cowboys and cops do like their coffee," he added as he sidestepped her energetic little boy and headed for the hot brew.

Her four year old was kicking a bright red ball and chasing it silently from aisle to aisle.

Why had Ingrid recoiled from his touch?

His head was starting to hurt.

He hated those damn headaches.

"You stop running, Winston." His mother said in broken English: "This place of business, not monster-boy playground."

Trick walked up to the counter and sat down his lidded cup of coffee. Jia Wong reached over to the register and rang up the sale. The sunlight glistened on the symbol she wore around her neck and caught his attention.

"That's pretty," Trick said, pointing to her necklace.

"Thank you," she said, nodding and toying with the chain. "Gift from Mr. Wong."

"What does the writing mean?"

"It say Good Fortune," she said, "symbol bring me luck."

"We can all use some of that. Where's Mr. Wong this morning?"

"He go to produce market early, before fresh be all gone."

Next time he saw Mr. Wong he'd ask him where he could buy a necklace like that for Ingrid. He wanted to please her.

Happy wife, happy life.

Why had she pulled away from him?

A loud crash startled them both. They turned to see little Winston had knocked over a free standing shelf. He sat on the floor covered in 99 cent bags of pretzel sticks, holding his red ball and looking bewildered. He still had to learn the laws of physics. You hit an object hard enough, it's going to tumble. You slam into something hard enough you're going to fall.

"Stupid, clumsy boy!" said Jia Wong.

"Hey, accidents happen, no harm done," Trick said, abandoning his coffee. He walked over to where the stunned boy sat on the floor next to the upended the rack. Trick lifting the rack and as he replaced the last bag onto its shelf Jia spoke up in her sharp, foreign cadence.

"Clumsy boy make big mess," she reprimanded from behind the counter.

The boy's lip began to quiver.

"It's okay, little man," Trick said, gently lifting the boy to his feet.

"Fortune has given me an idiot for a son. I am cursed with a boy who will never amount to anything."

Trick's headache was feeling worse. What had started as a throb burst into full bloom, a jackhammer reverberated through his temples and jabbed into his brain like a sharp, hot knife.

"It was an accident, Mrs. Wong," he said, rubbing his temples.

Young Winston looked up at his hero of the moment and smiled. Trick returned his smile and gave him a wink. Winston winked back and giggled.

"Mr. Wong should have given her the symbol for serenity," he mumbled under his breath.

As he exited through the front door he overheard her address her son.

"You shame me, Winston. Go in back room," she ordered. "I work now to put food in bad boy's rice bowl."

Trick Delgado coughed out the dusty desert air as he headed for his car, then spat onto the pavement. If Jia Wong didn't make such damn good coffee he'd have found another place to take his business.

Goddamn it, his head hurt.

He got into the car, reached into the glove compartment and took out a small pill bottle. He swallowed two migraine tablets and washed them down with Agua Verde's best cup of coffee. He shoved the key into the ignition, started the engine, turned into the glaring morning sun and headed for work.

SIX

"Where the hell is Delgado?" Chief Irwin roared as he looked around the squad room. The veins on his forehead visibly pulsated, his nose and ears glowing redder than the lights on a Christmas tree. "He was supposed to be here ten minutes ago, for Christ sakes."

As if on cue the door opened and Trick Delgado entered the room.

"You're late," said the Chief, a surly, silver haired man in his fifties with a hint of east coast accent and a strong, stubbled chin.

Trick looked at his watch. "I apologize sir, I must've lost track of the time."

Chief Irwin inhaled deeply, followed by an audible asthmatic squeak as he exhaled. He waved his hands and shook them as if they were wet, shoved them into his pockets and squared his shoulders.

"Sit, Delgado," he ordered.

Trick sat in the empty chair next to Big Jim Bullock.

It was a sorry excuse for a police headquarters. The small building housed the Chief's office, a desk filled main room where the officers conducted their business, when there was business to conduct. There was a bathroom with a shower stall, one holding cell plus another two cells where the drunks slept it off or the bad guys waited it out before being transferred to county jail. The cops were lucky to have phones and computers, but it was a sight better than last generation's two-room deserted store front on a dusty, unpaved road. There was an extra room which served as the squad room, interrogation room, conference room and monthly meeting place for the city council. What passed as a break room was Bad Sandy's Café next door. The adjoining building on the opposite side housed the chambers of Judge Gareth Lambert and the courthouse. Neither place saw much activity.

"Okay, let's get this show on the road. We've got more complaints about the graffiti. It's spreading faster than gonorrhea in a whorehouse. The punks are tagging storefronts and fences quicker than they can be painted over. For starters, we've asked Dorman's Hardware to put the spray paint under lock and key and not to sell it to anybody under twenty-one."

"They're not *all* kids," said Jim Bullock. "There's plenty of them out there who'll never grow up. Hell, we've got gang members pushing thirty."

"And all of 'em are keeping us in business," said Mackey Hogan.

The chief shrugged. "Yeah, I know. As if a lock will make much difference. Hell, it might at least slow 'em down. Just keep your eyes open and if you catch any of the little bastards cuff 'em and stuff 'em and haul in their sorry behinds."

Trick checked his watch again, then looked over to Jim.

"You with us, Delgado?" asked the Chief.

"Yes sir, graffiti sir," he responded as though he were still in Special Forces.

The formality of Trick's response made the Chief crack a hint of a smile. It was beyond him why someone with Trick's smarts, not to mention his stellar military record, would choose to stay in Agua Verde. With his training in Special Forces he could've written his own ticket out of town.

To call the station casual was an understatement. It was difficult to keep it otherwise with just five officers and an overworked police chief. The lines blurred with no strict adherence to chain of command. Everything overlapped and they did their best, which wasn't bad under the circumstances.

If a bond issue came up for more funding it was voted down; a near-sighted populace found a trolley, that went up and down three measly blocks of downtown rails, preferable to their own protection. They were content with a volunteer fire department and potholed roads, as long as they had their bike lanes and community vegetable garden and a farmer's market on Saturday mornings. A shit hole of a town straining to look hip, Chief Irwin figured Agua Verde's younger generation got what it deserved.

"So what are we looking for, Chief?" asked Mackey Hogan. "Can we haul in the skin heads and gang bangers? The wetbacks and coons?"

Chief Irwin bristled. "Anybody you catch *in the act*, Mackey. I don't care if they're white or green or somebody's granny. And neither should you." He looked Mackey up and down. "And button up your shirt. You look like an unmade bed."

Mackey flattened his wayward chest hair and buttoned his top button.

"You're a racist son-of-a-bitch, Mackey," said Trick.

Their one black cop squirmed uncomfortably in his chair, but said nothing. William Washington was a transplant from Detroit, square-shouldered and proud. Detroit had been home to the Washington family for generations. His grandfather had pulled them up from poverty with a good factory job and William's father had followed in his footsteps. One by one the factories closed and the residents of 8 Mile learned to live on less and less. But his father had instilled in his son a work ethic and dignity. William had joined the Detroit force only to see 8 Mile and the people in it deteriorate until the streets were in ruins and the people had replaced hope with anger. Half of them were drugged up and itching for a fight while the rest silently carried the weight of their broken dreams on stooped shoulders. Unlike his father who'd found another job at half the pay, they lived on government hand-outs until all ambition was gone. Getting something for nothing had become a way of life until they couldn't see beyond the government check and food stamps in the mail box. Or the drugs that numbed them into indifference.

William's father had said, "You can't have a big appetite in someone else's refrigerator."

He'd taken that advice to heart, worked hard and kept his nose clean, believing that one made his own opportunities regardless of the obstacles. One day he'd been driving through 8 Mile, looking at the crumbling buildings, deserted businesses and broken people. It was like watching a beautiful woman die, then having to stand there and watch as the corpse rotted. The people he was paid to protect had surrounded themselves with an invisible barbed wire fence and couldn't see their way out.

But he could.

That one homicide damn nearly destroyed him. He'd had enough.

He turned in his badge, headed west and tried to leave that memory in Detroit.

William Washington. Not Billy. Not Bill. Not Will or Willy. He insisted on being called William, seeing the formality as a sign of respect. And he demanded respect.

"Jesus Christ, you're a sorry lot," said the Chief. "Any questions before we get out of here?"

The sound of a rooster crowing broke the silence.

"What the—?"

Cock-a-doodle-doo.

Snickers, followed by all-out laughter filled the room.

"Crap, sorry sir," said Trick as he reached into his pocket and pulled out his cell phone. "I forgot to turn it off, Chief."

"Cute ring tone," Mackey smirked.

Trick ignored him as he looked down to see who was calling, disconnected, and shoved it back into his pocket. It was the last person he wanted to talk to.

With an impatient wave, Chief Irwin dismissed them and one by one they filed out. William Washington shot a look that could kill in the direction of Mackey Hogan.

"Why don't you say something, or do something, when Mackey talks like that?" Jim Bullock asked.

"Because that's what he wants."

"But still..."

"I've seen a thirteen year old with a bullet in his head because someone perceived he'd been disrespected. Words are nothing but words and I refuse to let Mackey get to me. If I gave in to it he'd suffer the same fate, believe me."

Before Jim Bullock reached the door, Trick motioned him aside.

"Quite a show you put on, Trick." Big Jim smiled.

"Yeah, I guess I'm a little distracted this morning."

"No harm, no foul."

"Right. It's not like any of us are worried about getting shit-canned, that's for sure. Let's go over to Bad Sandy's where we can talk."

"Sounds serious," said Jim following him out the door and into Bad Sandy's Café. They slid into a duct taped red vinyl booth against the back wall.

"No, no, nothing dramatic at all. Ingrid and I were talking this morning and she mentioned it's been awhile. Anyway, we'd like you to come over for dinner Saturday. Lately we haven't had much of a chance to just kick back and relax."

"It'd do us all some good," said Jim, thinking about the troublesome little rescue waiting for him back home. Paco had only been there a day and Jim was already looking for a break. "Want me to bring my special? Or just a six-pack?"

"Beer suits me fine, but Ingrid never stops raving about your special cheesecake. Says you're a damn sight better in the kitchen than she is."

"I'll bring both."

Sandy walked over and handed them sticky menus. He was a big man with a shaved head, his arms and neck filled with second-rate prison tats and scarred fingers with hairy knuckles. His body was a roadmap of his troubled past. He was the owner, the chef and the server all rolled into one and living proof that a hardcore ex-con could actually go straight if he put enough sweat and determination into it. But opening a business next to the police station showed that his balls were as big as they'd been in the joint. No one would have believed his best patrons would be the cops who'd chosen it for their hangout. Hell, it was convenient and they liked to think that their presence helped keep Sandy on the straight and narrow. Trick's wife Ingrid would have said he chose the spot next to the police station as a crutch. It was his safety-net just in case he ever got tempted to go back to his old ways. Trick would have said Sandy just didn't like being a big man living in a little box.

"Just coffee," said Trick.

"Same here," said Jim. Sandy wrote it down and walked away. He never was a big talker.

"So it's set then?" Trick asked.

"What?"

"Saturday night."

"In stone. Thanks for the invite. Time flies, that's for sure. The older we get the faster it flies. Pretty soon we'll be sitting in rocking chairs comparing our aches and pains and talking about the good old days."

"If we're lucky enough to live that long."

"And lucky enough to have some good old days to look back on."

Head lowered, Trick Delgado traced his fingertip along the beading moisture on his water glass, like a kid who just got caught at something he knew he shouldn't have done.

"Uh, one more thing."

"What?"

"Okay," he hesitated. "Ingrid's at it again."

Jim groaned. "Oh please, not another fix-up."

"She likes you Jim. And she's determined. She doesn't think anybody's happy unless they're paired off."

"You know how I feel."

"I know. You'd rather fly solo, but Ingrid says this one's a looker. And smart. How bad could it be?"

"Sounds like you're on her side."

"Better on her side than not. You know how a woman is once she gets an idea in her head."

Jim was Ingrid's pet project. Her incessant match-making was the last thing he wanted to deal with, but he'd run out of ways to dodge her cupid's arrows.

And some of her questions.

"You okay then?"

"Oh, what the hell." Then added: "Who knows? This might be the one, right?" But there was no conviction in his voice.

"Happy wife, happy life," said Trick. It was an expression he repeated often, like his own special mantra. "Ingrid makes me happier than a kid on Christmas so I'm not going to fuck up this one, but shit Jim, sometimes I swear if we weren't married she'd be going after you."

"You're safe," said Jim. "You two are made for each other."

"If she went after you, could I arrest her for stalking?"

Bad Sandy walked over and topped off their coffee.

"Sandy," said Trick. "Why on earth did you call this place BAD Sandy's?"

"I dunno," he shrugged. "Mama always said I was a bad seed. And I've got the rap sheet that proved her right."

"But now you've proved her wrong," said Jim, waving his arm to indicate the little café that had finally steered Sandy into a crime free life.

Sandy shrugged and headed back to the kitchen. He was a man of few words.

The two cops talked as they casually drank their coffee, then rose, waved goodbye to Bad Sandy and walked out the door into the rising heat.

Big Jim and Trick walked off in opposite directions. Jim got into his car and steered his way out of the parking lot and into the day, while Trick pulled his cell phone from his pocket, leaned against his car, punched in a number and put it on speaker. Might as well get it over with.

"You're not supposed to call me at work."

"Twinkie's out of treats," she said. "I need some cat food."

"That's hardly an emergency."

"What? You want my poor baby to starve? Would that make you happy?"

"Mom, mom, mom!"

"Well?"

"Why the hell can't you go to the store yourself?"

"Don't you cuss at me, Patrick Delgado. I didn't raise you to have potty mouth." She'd spat out his last name like it tasted nasty in her mouth. "You know I don't drive."

"Don't call me Patrick, you know I hate that. The store's two blocks. Why don't you walk? The fresh air would do you some good."

"In my condition? You want to kill me too? And Patrick's a good name. An Irish name. He was a blessed Saint, although I can't say much of his benevolence rubbed off on you."

The only condition Trick's mother had was in her head, but there was no sense arguing with her. About anything. Ever.

It was no win every time.

"I'll pick some up after work. I've got to go."

"Twinkie could starve by then."

"Forever the martyr, Mom. Just give her a can of fucking people tuna." He disconnected the phone before she could respond.

He got into the car and reached into the glove compartment, pulled out the pill bottle and dry-swallowed two more migraine tablets. She only called him Patrick when she wanted to piss him off. It always worked. And it always gave him a blasting headache.

Women. They were a curse. He was convinced God was a woman, despite his Catholic upbringing. A vengeful Goddess. Three ex-wives who didn't know how to be wives and a mother who was no typical mother. You'd have never found her wearing an apron or baking a pie or tucking him in at bedtime when he was little. But he loved her. After all was said and done, she was his mother and he was her only child. When his father walked out on them she'd raised him alone. That counted for something even if it had put her in a permanent sour mood.

The most trivial of things could trigger her Celtic wrath, whether it was a fly that got in the house, a stain that wouldn't come out, a dented can, or an instruction sheet written in Spanish as well as English. Items would fly through the air at warp speed and with enough momentum that she could have out-pitched Roger Clemens. Clemens once said: “Everybody kind of perceives me as being angry. It’s not anger, it’s motivation.” His mother had one up on Roger. Anger *was* her motivation, so Trick learned early on how to duck like a dodge-ball king. He’d still received plenty of direct hits, but managed to avert his share. All that practice had made him downright agile on the playground, so he figured there was an up side to just about anything. Even her frequent blows to his head.

She’d always been pissed off at something. Or angry at nothing at all. What were once nice features now reflected her black Irish heart. The years etched a brittleness across her face and dug scowl lines into deep furrows. As she stood before the mirror masked in makeup, it could no longer lie to her. Trick found that sad, like a forgotten flower wilted in a vase of rancid water. He decided to be nicer to her, even if it meant walking on egg shells in her presence.

Women.

Despite a run of bad luck with the ladies, despite all their quirks and mysteries, Trick Delgado loved women. And with Ingrid, he’d finally loved one who loved him back.

SEVEN

The sun was doing a nosedive behind the purple mountains by the time Big Jim Bullock pulled into his driveway. The day had been uneventful. A few speeding tickets and not much else. Impatient travelers were easy pickings and helped to fill the town coffers as they sped towards some unknown destination. Agua Verde was a town that people went through, not to. There was nothing here worth staying for any longer than it took to down a quick lunch or top off the tank before heading back onto the road. Uneventful was good, but he doubted he could say as much for what awaited him.

Paco was probably still sitting in the chair where he'd left him pouting, waiting for his *Chim* to come home. He wasn't sure if the little squirt enjoyed playing helpless or if he truly was. He was complicating things, but if Jim hadn't taken him in where would he be? Wandering the streets with a cast on his leg wondering why his rescuing angel had abandon him? The kid had already been through enough. Jim grabbed the grocery bag from the passenger seat, the oddly colored mystery meat called chorizo, hot sauce and a couple dozen eggs, and headed for the door.

The door flew open before he could shove the key into the lock.

"*Señor* Chim, you have come home!" If Paco were a puppy he'd have been wagging his tail.

"Well, look at you," said Jim. "I see you've learned to manage that heavy cast."

Paco limped behind him as Jim walked into the house. He could hear his old, scratched Xavier Cougat vinyl playing in the background.

"Look, look what I have done," said Paco, pointing proudly. The dining room table was meticulously set for two. A vase sat in the center of the table, filled with simple yellow flowers. "I walked outside and picked them for you. Does their sunshine make you happy?"

Jim looked at the blooms from the brittle bush plant and smiled. Paco had worked very hard and his efforts had actually made his house feel more like a home, whether for himself or Paco or both of them was of no consequence. It had created a sense of warmth and welcome he hadn't felt for a very long time.

"Very happy," he said, looking at the linen tablecloth that had lived in the hall closet forgotten and unused. Normally his dinner for one sat on his lap while he relaxed in the recliner watching the day's news and unwinding.

"This morning I could see you were not happy with me. I am sorry as I want your happiness. I was bad, but I promise I will be better."

"And I could've been more patient."

"Look, come look at this," Paco said, hobbling to the living room.

Jim's art books were strewn across the floor and around the recliner.

"The books are beautiful and I looked at every one. I am in love with the artist *Klumpet!"*

"Klumpet?" Jim was puzzled.

"*Si,* Klumpet," he repeated, pointing at the book that sat in the recliner.

Jim looked down at the book on Gustav Klimpt, his famous painting of The Kiss on the cover, and smiled. "Good taste."

"And when I brought in the newspaper I saw this," he said, reaching for the newspaper and thumbing to a page. "There is an art show and look, there is a picture of a painting. I like that painting, Chim. Very much. I've never seen an art show. Can we go? Can we?"

He shoved the paper into Jim's face. Jim sat his grocery bag on the floor, took the paper from him and read where Paco had pointed.

"Doobie," he said. "I've been to his exhibits before. He's good. Makes me wonder why he landed here."

"Can we go? Can we?"

"Can you get around on that leg?"

"To see this I would happily crawl through cactus and a thousand fire ants."

Big Jim Bullock was impressed with Paco's enthusiasm. Besides, the gallery was a place where he'd never run into co-workers. Their tastes ran more to the local watering holes and strip joints. Paco had somehow zeroed in on the one place in town that Jim frequented and loved.

"So you like art?" It had definitely distracted the waif from focusing on his clumsy leg cast and his world of sorrow. That alone was worth something.

"Art like this I have never seen, Chim. In our *casa* we had photos of our *familia* and many pictures of the saints and the blessed virgin. They were pretty, but not like this. The only other art I've seen is on the sides of buildings." He jabbed the newspaper with his finger. "The story was hard for me to read in the English, but it says Friday."

"Then Friday night it is," said Jim. "I'll introduce you to the artist."

"You know a real artist?"

Paco used his good leg to pivot himself around in circles as he squealed like an off-key Mariachi singer.

EIGHT

The following morning started badly. Especially for the body that lay on it's back on the linoleum floor behind the counter, crumpled like a rag doll that had been carelessly tossed aside. There was no blood and there were no signs of violence, except for the broken neck that set her pose at an unnatural angle and a wrenched arm with a delicate, ochre-hued hand reaching toward the ceiling.

Mr. Wong was in shock and choked back the tears as he spoke with the officers.

"I come downstairs and find her like this, my beautiful Jia."

"Were there any customers in the store when you got here?" asked Trick. The way the body lay behind the counter it could easily have gone unnoticed. The one morning he'd skipped stopping in for his coffee and disaster hit. If he'd been there it might not have happened. As irrational as the thought was, it made him feel somehow responsible. The Wong's had been welcomed as part of the town as soon as they'd legally immigrated from China after years of waiting and red tape, unlike a few of the trouble makers that wrote their own tickets across the southern border by dark of night. Some were okay and looked for work and a chance at better life, but the bad ones just looked for trouble and added to the chaos.

The Wong's were good people.

"No, except for my son. But Winston was in back room playing."

"Where is he now?" asked Trick.

"I make him stay in back. This he must not see."

"Of course not," said Trick, remembering the energetic child that ran yesterday's aisles, creating chaos for his mother. He was hoping the boy hadn't witnessed the violence. Even if he had seen something, Trick doubted he'd be much help. Kids that young had a way of blending reality with fantasy. In questioning them, asking a question the wrong way could lead them and they'd say what they thought you wanted to hear. They had vivid imaginations and were unreliable little buggers at best. But it wouldn't hurt to ask a question or two, just in case.

"I'd like to speak with him."

"Don't tell him what happened," begged Mr. Wong.

Trick turned back to Jim before Mr. Wong led him into the back room.

"We'll be a few minutes," he said. "You might as well get the kit and start dusting for prints."

With boxes of merchandise stacked to the ceiling and stairs that led to a second level, the remaining floor space wasn't much bigger than a bedroom. The back entrance was locked from the inside, which indicated that wasn't the point of entry. Whoever did this walked right through the front door. The boy looked up from where he sat on the floor coloring in his coloring book.

"Coffee man," he said with a smile, recognizing the officer. "Cowboys and cops like coffee, not tea."

The boy has big ears, thought Trick, remembering his last, short exchange with Mrs. Wong. Quiet as Winston was he didn't miss much.

"Hi there, little fella. I'm happy to see you again. Where's your red ball?"

"I'm coloring now so I put it in the toy box. One toy at a time only."

Mrs. Wong must've had rules to cover every move the boy made. Some kind of control freak. Trick's wife Ingrid might have diagnosed her as having obsessive/compulsive disorder. He wondered if she tossed orders to Mr. Wong the same way. An interesting dynamic as he appeared, in contrast to his wife, a docile soul. Someone as controllable as a child. There was little doubt Jia Wong had been the iron fist of the family.

"Coffee, not tea," Winston repeated.

He was certainly more talkative around his father than when his mother was present.

Mr. Wong lifted the boy into his arms.

"He just wants to talk to you for a minute," said the father as he held him. "He needs to ask you a few questions."

"Did I do bad?"

"No, of course not," said his father, kissing him on the forehead.

"Do you know where your mother is?" Trick considered that a safe start, an opening for him to volunteer had he seen something. Could he have seen what happened? Would he even have understood if he had? Or had he been safely admonished to the back as usual?

"She's in front making money to feed bad boy."

"You're not a bad boy, Winston. You're a very good boy and you're going to grow up to be a very wise man."

Mr. Wong smiled at Trick's comment.

"Me?" Winston asked, breaking into a grin.

"Yes, you're very special."

If Winston could have grinned any wider the corners of his mouth would have hit his earlobes.

"Special," he repeated. "Very good boy."

"You are most gentle with children," said Mr. Wong. "My Winston can be shy, but I see he likes you."

"I love kids."

"You have children?" He was relieved to change the subject. It was a momentary distraction from the tragedy that lay in the other room.

"No, so far I haven't been that lucky."

"A child brings happiness to a home, like a lotus blossom brings beauty to a pond."

"You are blessed with a wonderful child." Trick sensed his next words would sound empty, but he was compelled to say them. "And I'm truly sorry for your loss."

"I thank you for your kind words. I only hope that Winston's joy will help me through my sorrow."

Trick looked over at the staircase.

"What's up there, more storage?"

"We live on second floor."

It would be difficult to ask the man to leave the store until the investigation was over. It wasn't just his place of business, but also his home. It wouldn't be fair to disrupt the little boy's life any more than necessary. And Mr. Wong had a difficult task ahead of him trying to find the right words to tell him why his mother was gone forever. Trick motioned for him to return Winston to his coloring. Mr. Wong sat him back on the floor.

"You stay here, Winston," he said.

"Yes, *bába*."

The two men returned to the front. Trick observed that Jim had finished dusting for and lifting prints. A forensics man wasn't in the town's budget. When necessary the department would send evidence to the county for analysis. The small stuff they handled themselves. The counter and refrigeration case panels held traces of dust as did the glass entry door and the counter where the coffee urn and soft drink machine sat. They'd likely be sifting through the prints of every customer who'd ever entered the place. He could see Jim outside putting up yellow tape as a small group of people gathered along the sidewalk. When he finished, he came back inside and started taking photographs of the crime scene.

"Let's wind this up quickly," said Trick. "They live upstairs and I don't want to inconvenience them more than we have to. Mr. Wong has enough to deal with."

"That's do-able," he replied, as the camera clicked away and captured images from every corner and angle.

"You got any security cameras?" Trick asked Mr. Wong.

"One."

"We'll need the tape."

Mr. Wong walked behind the counter, averting his eyes from the lifeless body of his wife as he pulled out a step stool, stood on the top rung and stretched his arm to the highest shelf. The camera was hidden among the more expensive bottles of whiskey and scotch, tilted down towards the cash register. He ejected the old vhs tape from the out-dated machine. "Odd," he said, looking at it. "This looks like a brand new tape but tape wasn't changed. Not full yet." He shrugged. "Mrs. Wong must have put in a new one this morning."

He got down from the stool and placed it back in the corner.

"We'll need to take that tape with us," said Jim Bullock. "And the last one that was removed."

Mr. Wong handed him the tape. Jim looked at it, discouraged. The clarity on those old tapes were mediocre at best compared to the new, updated systems. But they didn't come cheap.

Mr. Wong reached under the counter where the used tapes were kept. He removed the one at the top of the stack and looked at it. "This should be the last one, but it isn't. There is one missing."

"We'll take it, just in case."

"You need to find who did this to my Jia."

"We'll do our best," said Trick. "Is anything else missing? Have you checked the cash register?"

Mr. Wong was looking down at his wife's body and moaning.

"Mr. Wong, does it look like anything is missing?"

"Sorry," he said as he walked over and hit the key on the cash register. The drawer kicked open with a loud ring.

"Money is still here," he shrugged.

"That makes no sense," said Jim. "Why would anyone want to kill her if it wasn't a robbery?"

Mr. Wong looked around at the shelves, checking his inventory. He slowly walked up and down the aisles where Winston liked to kick his red ball, then back to where the two cops stood.

"Cigarettes," he finally said. "Many cartons gone. Half of beer case is empty. Someone would kill my Jia for beer and cigarettes?" He started to sob. "Why? Stupid, stupid, stupid! My Jia would have given them what they wanted. No trouble. No reason to hurt her."

Mr. Wong looked into Trick's eyes. "You find who did this."

The ambulance pulled up and two attendants entered. Jim motioned them to where the body lay.

Mr. Wong rushed over toward his wife's body, as if to protect her. Or to embrace her one last time. He stopped abruptly.

"Officer!" he called.

Trick walked over to where he stood.

"What is it?"

"One more thing is missing. Jia's beautiful necklace is not around her neck. She wore it all the time. It was my special gift to her and it is gone."

Trick looked down at the woman's body. That Good Fortune symbol sure as hell didn't bring her any luck, he thought as he pulled out his pen and scribbled more information on his notebook. He hoped it would show up at a pawn shop, providing him a lead. He wanted whoever did this to be caught and brought to justice. And he wanted to be the man to do it. As he shut the notebook, Mr. Wong took a step towards his wife, arms outstretched, muttering her name over and over.

"You'll have to step back, sir." said one of the attendants. Mr. Wong stared at him, a spark of anger surfacing in his confused eyes.

"I'm sorry, but it's important you not disturb the crime scene."

He bowed, then stepped back and turned away.

There was a finality to the zipping sound, like a slamming door, as they enclosed her in the black body bag, then gently lifted her onto the stretcher and out the door.

Mr. Wong walked over to Jim and whispered, "When may I have my wife back?"

"Soon."

"Where are they taking her?"

Jim wanted to cry right along with the man. They'd have to question Mr. Wong in more detail, but that could wait for later. The spouse is always suspect number one, but one look at him and Jim could see the genuine pain in his eyes. How could he tell the man diplomatically that they were taking his wife to be cut up in autopsy before he'd see her again? Shit, he hated this part of the job. How could one soften the facts of something so invasive and brutal?

"We need to look for clues, possible DNA, anything that might lead to finding who murdered her. I'm sorry. We'll contact you as soon as her—as soon as she can be released."

The two cops turned towards the door.

"Wait one moment please," said Mr. Wong.

He turned and went into the back room. He came back holding a large, white cloth in one hand and a hammer and nails in the other. He accompanied the officers through the front door and as they walked to the parking lot, Big Jim looked back to see Mr. Wong nailing the white cloth above the front of the shop. It billowed in the hot desert breeze and draped down to cover the top half of the door. There was something solemn and ritualistic and mysterious in Mr. Wong's gesture.

Trick looked at the small crowd gathered beyond the barrier.

Step one of the investigation was completed, so he stomped over and started ripping down the yellow crime scene tape.

"Why don't you people show Mr. Wong some respect and go back where you came from?"

"It wasn't Wong in the body bag?" one of the onlookers asked.

"It was his wife."

There was an audible gasp from the curious choir.

"What happened?" asked another.

"It was a robbery. Now get the fuck out of here and leave the man in peace."

One by one the crowd dispersed, and one by one they looked back over their shoulders as they walked away.

"They're more shameless than rubber-neckers sniffing for blood at a traffic accident," said Trick.

"Human nature."

"It's ghoulish."

"Things like this damn near break my heart," said Jim. "It's hard to stay tough. And even harder trying to make sense out of something so senseless."

"It stinks," said Trick. "At least we don't have to deal with it very often."

"Once is once too many."

"This is the first time that it touched me personally. The first time the victim wasn't a total stranger. It puts a different spin on things," said Trick.

One of his headaches was surfacing. He rubbed his temples, squinted his brow.

"You really ought to see a doc about those headaches."

"I have. She gave me a prescription for migraine pills."

"Do they help?"

"If I ignore the label and swallow enough of them. Even better if I can down them with a can of beer or some good whiskey." He laughed, then self-consciously shoved his hands into his pockets. "The one morning I didn't have time to stop for coffee and this happens. If I'd come, do you—?"

"No, I don't think it would have made a difference."

"You believe in predestination?"

"I believe some things just happen. If we had a crystal ball we could prevent it, but we don't."

"So we're the clean up crew."

"As good a job description as any. But now we find out who the son-of-a-bitch was."

"I'm going to miss Mrs. Wong."

"How well did you know her, Trick?"

"Well enough to know she made the best damn cup of coffee in Agua Verde."

Mr. Wong came out of the door again, this time carrying tools, a ladder, and a gong. He climbed the ladder and screwed the gong to the right of the door. He hit the gong with a small mallet before he stepped down from the ladder. The gong made a deep, mournful sound that echoed across the parking lot and down the sidewalk. His shoulders were drooped in defeat as he reentered the building and flipped the sign on the glass door to read: CLOSED.

NINE

Paco had looked forward to this night with the enthusiasm of a child waiting for Christmas morning. Big Jim Bullock was taking him to a real art show in a real gallery and Paco wasn't going to let his cumbersome cast slow him down, not one bit. His determination had surprised his rescuer and he could see the relief in Jim's eyes every time he took another step forward and did more for himself, relying less and less on Jim. It wasn't easy. He loved Jim doing things for him. He loved being pampered. It made him feel, for the first time in a long time, as if someone cared. He had come to see himself as a pariah that no one wanted, visualizing himself dying by a dumpster in some dark alley and being unceremoniously scooped up and removed with the rest of the trash.

But Big Jim Bullock had come along and saved him. And showed him that he had worth. Paco didn't want to disappoint him.

"I can do this," he said as Jim opened the car door, offering his hand to help. It wasn't easy but Paco slid into the passenger seat, being sure to make just enough grunts and groans to elicit a bit of sympathy as he swung his bad leg awkwardly into the car. Jim ignored his dramatics, slammed the passenger door and got into the driver's seat. The deep orange sun dipped behind the mountains as they headed for the gallery and their first night out since Jim had taken Paco under his wing.

* * * *

Doobie the artist had arrived at the gallery early, as was expected of him, dressed in his usual beatnik black. He wore a chip on his shoulder and six stiff drinks under his belt. Old habits die hard. He hated galleries. He hated the politics and greed, the evil necessity of a process that devoured creative spirit in exchange for food on the table. He hated openings most of all—having to chat up the common herd—answer stupid questions of the pompous uninformed who drove over from Phoenix or Tucson. They saw non-existent symbolism and hidden meaning behind his every brush stroke. Bullshit and bombast. Doobie was oblivious to the fact that he was equally as pretentious as his followers. Or that if it wasn't for them he'd be hard put to sell anything. Agua Verde wasn't known for full pockets.

The first customer through the door was Big Jim Bullock. Despite his never having bought a painting, he was one person Doobie looked forward to seeing. The big policeman was a welcome sight. Back in his old stomping grounds Doobie would have been racing to flush his stash down the toilet, but here in Agua Verde he'd found a cop who didn't fit the mold. It was refreshing but their friendship remained comfortably within the gallery walls. Old opinions died hard but Jim was a hell of a lot better than the would-be art snobs that came to his shows, who worked hard at impressing others as well as themselves.

They brought in the bucks, but they bored him.

Doobie reeled across the room, drink in hand to where Jim stood with a little waif at his side. The young man had a cast on one leg, but as he walked he managed to move like a ballet dancer with the other in a clomp/pirouette sort of motion. He was as gay as a bead-clad marcher at Mardi Gras and flaunted it proudly.

"Jim, good to see you."

"Paco, this is the Doobie. Doobie, Paco."

Paco was in awe as the two shook hands. He'd never met a real artist before.

Jim saw a definite question mark on Doobie's face.

"Paco is my cousin," he lied. "He's visiting from San Antonio."

"Welcome to Agua Verde," said Doobie. "Enjoy the show."

"*Si,*" he said. "This is *muey* exciting."

"How'd you hurt that leg?" Doobie asked, trying to make small talk as he took a gulp of his wine and wiped his mouth.

Before Paco could get the words out Jim interrupted.

"He's a rodeo clown." Where the hell did that come from, he thought. It sounded stupid, even to himself. "Dangerous profession," he added in explanation.

"More dangerous than yours, by the looks of it."

Paco looked at him, confused, but Jim's little lie served the purpose. Some things were no one else's business. The gallery was the one place in Agua Verde where Jim could relax and he intended to keep it that way. Doobie could smell cop on him and Jim could smell pot on Doobie, so their 'Don't ask, don't tell' was mutually beneficial.

"That wine's tempting," Jim changed the subject as Doobie drained his glass.

"There's more where this came from," he said.

Jim headed for the wine bar as Paco flitted from painting to painting like a hyper kid at Toys R Us, gasping his admiration in a staccato of Spanish and English. A woman sidled up to Jim, catching his eye and flirting shamelessly through a bucket of sloppily applied make-up. Her hair was a drab shade of premature gray that framed her even paler complexion, but for the rouge that kissed her sagging cheeks. Heavy ethnic jewelry hung around her neck like a noose fashioned from a tow chain and the weight of her earrings pulled down her lobes giving her the appearance of a floppy-eared rabbit. By the red marbling in her bloodshot eyes she must have been downing the wine in record time. Probably one of the locals who came in for the free wine and hors d'ouvres. She hardly struck him as a connoisseur of the finer arts and her taste for wine was probably as unsophisticated as her gaudy wardrobe. Had she been a painting she'd have been splashed together half-hazardously by the likes of Jackson Pollack.

"My name's Tammy."

"It suits you," he said. An image flashed through his mind. Tammy Lee Baker, the fallen preacher's wife, who'd cried rivers of black mascara for the news cameras.

"It's an impressive show, don't you think?" she asked, tossing her long hair and reaching for the cheese platter. She popped a square of Gouda into her mouth and chewed on it unceremoniously. She smiled, bits of red cheese rind clinging to her teeth. "He's a mah-velous artist."

"I don't know how he does it. I don't have a creative bone in my body." Jim turned away from her and took a sip of his wine.

"Your body looks fine to me," she said with a smile. "I'll bet a handsome man like you is full of surprises."

"Chim, Chim! This one, this one," Paco squealed from across the room.

"You'll have to excuse me," he said, making no attempt to mask his relief.

Jim gulped down his Merlot as he walked over and stood before the painting. Bold colors, unlike the wispy, watery weak flowers painted by old ladies desperate to fill their empty hours. Doobie had taught him to appreciate what watercolors could be. He liked their strength and perfection and boldness. The subject was never flowers. Doobie preferred cars and trolleys and architecture. Paco had made a good choice, an accomplishment for a kid whose only exposure to art had been the graffiti that tagged the barrio.

And Jim's art books.

Buying books on art was cheaper than collecting the real thing.

Jim was proud of him.

"Oh, and this one," said Paco. "And this one, too. Please?"

"One, Paco. Choose just one."

How could he say no when Paco couldn't decide? He bought him all three.

Jim took out his checkbook and cringed as his bank balance diminished before his eyes. Customers lined up behind him, anxious to make their own purchases. The walls were emptying fast and Jim overheard the gallery owner address Doobie:

"There's not much choice," the man said. "We don't have enough works left to keep the show going and we've just opened the doors. Look at the walls for chrissakes."

"I'm not a fucking machine that you can turn on at the flip of a switch."

"Don't go prima donna on me, Doobie. You should be thrilled that we need more paintings. Or do you prefer the show come to a screeching halt?"

Doobie was used to success and tonight had been unusually profitable, but it left him with no alternative than to cough up more paintings. Fast. He didn't like painting under pressure. It took the fun out of it and turned it into work. And he didn't like work.

God, but he hated the business side of things.

"Give me a week," he snapped and headed back to the wine bar to refill his glass.

TEN

Trick Delgado's guts were doing acrobatics. He hated confrontation. He was running late. Ingrid was pissed when he'd called and said don't hold dinner. Her words stabbed sharp as shivs in a prison exercise yard. She topped them with the usual accusations regarding his mother. She'd called him a mama's boy, said that as long as the old bitch came first she came in second. She was right that Peggy was an old bitch, but the rest wasn't true. Ingrid would always be number one. But he had an obligation. He'd made a promise. He'd get home as soon as he could. Their brief exchange didn't calmed his nerves or ease her disappointment.

A mother was supposed to be a soft place to land, but Peggy Delgado was more like diving head first into a briar batch. He took a deep breath then walked into his mother's house, holding a bag full of groceries in each arm. He dropped them onto the kitchen table with a thud and looked over at his mother who stood in front of the refrigerator, arms crossed stubbornly in front of her, while her orange cat Twinkie wrapped himself around her ankles.

"It's about time," said Peggy Delgado. "You should have been here yesterday. My Twinkie is starving. And be careful. You probably broke some of the eggs dropping the bag down like that." She walked over and reached into the bag, taking out the egg carton and opening it. One by one she wiggled them in their little oval nests, testing until she found what she needed to prove her point. "There," she said. "Just like I told you. One is cracked." She held it up, an expression of victory washing across her face. "Did you remember Twinkie's food?" She shoved her arm into the bag, feeling the contents with her fingers. "It figures, you always forget something."

"Look in the other bag, Ma." He wasn't going to let her get to him.

She dumped out the contents of the other bag, disappointment curling down the corners of her mouth as the cans of cat food rolled across the table.

"A thank you would be nice," he said.

"Don't be Mr. Smart Mouth with me," she said. "A good son takes care of his mother."

And a good mother loves her son, Trick thought as he pulled out a chair and sat down, watching as his ungrateful mother sorted through the groceries. She opened a can of cat food, shook the contents into a bowl and sat it on the floor for Twinkie. It was as if Trick wasn't even there.

"I need to go now," he said.

"You just got here, Patrick," she said, a hint of sweetness in her tone.

"Don't call me that. You know I hate it."

"That's the name you were baptized with and it's the only good thing you got from my side."

Trick's headache started up again. He rubbed his temples.

"You'd be better off if you got more of the Irish genes and fewer of the Mexican."

She'd replayed that one over and over for as far back as he could remember. As if he had any control over who he was. As if it were his fault that she'd picked a loser to father her only child. The man's ethnicity had nothing to do with it. He'd have been a poor choice if his ancestors had come over on the Mayflower. She hadn't been the first girl to have her common sense blinded by youth and hormones and she wouldn't be the last. But you couldn't tell her that. She chose to see herself as a wronged saint. In her scenario it was all that wily south of the border Cassanova's fault. Her role in life had become that of the perpetual victim.

"Ingrid would say you have misplaced anger..."

"Wife number...I've lost count," she said sarcastically. "She doesn't know me. She'll never understand what I've endured."

Ever the Irish martyr, he thought to himself, wise enough to keep his mouth shut. The years had taught the lesson well. Confronting her was always a mistake. It wasn't worth it. Her mouth could spit out words faster than a Gatling gun, words that were coated in barbed wire and cut deep enough to make his brain bleed. At least that's what it felt like, as if she'd stabbed an ice pick into his head then gleefully ground it around until it reached the very core of his being. Her words hurt as bad as her fists, maybe more. At least she didn't use those mighty fists any more. Her little boy had become bigger and stronger and was no longer a safe target. So her words had become her weapon of choice but they proved just as lethal.

"Let's play nice, okay?" He reached into his pocket for his headache pills, his sweet little saviors, shook the bottle and popped two into his mouth.

"Patri—" She caught herself. "You don't want water with those, *Trick*?"

"Thanks, no." His brain felt like Gene Kruppa was in there, pounding the drums through amplifiers. It hurt like blazes.

"Another headache?" Her voice was an unemotional monotone, playing him, pretending she actually gave a shit.

"Yeah, I've got to get going."

"I wish you'd stay. I get lonely."

Always her mixed messages. He wasn't about to fall for the Catholic guilt, not this time.

All he ever wanted was her approval. For her to say she was proud of him. For the damn headaches to go away. The gods weren't listening and he doubted they ever would. He rose from his chair and kissed her on her crepe paper cheek.

"Just like his father, Twinkie," he heard her say as he walked out the door.

* * * *

Trick Delgado lay in bed staring at the back of his wife's head. The cadence of Ingrid's breathing said she was only pretending to be asleep. It bothered him that she was shutting him out. It bothered him that something was bothering her and he didn't know what it was.

He hoped to hell it wasn't him.

"I know you're awake," he said.

Ingrid stretched her body like a cat and turned to face him.

"I'm not in the mood."

"Are you in the mood to talk?"

"No."

"Why are you acting like this?"

Ingrid reached across and turned on the night stand lamp. It formed a shimmering halo of soft gold around her pale blonde hair as she sat up against the pillow and stared him down.

"Is it me?" he asked. "Did I do something wrong?"

Her silence was deafening. She tried hard to keep her emotions locked safely inside. They needed to come out and smell the fresh air. Things never seemed so bad once they were verbalized, they both knew that. It was part of their dance. She couldn't help herself. This part of her character was as deeply imbedded as a fossil in sedimentary rock and nothing less than a hammer and sharp chisel could free it. On the few occasions when she opened up she expressed herself with abandon and they both felt better for it. It was a contradictory juggling act and he did his did his best to catch the ball at the right time. He wiggled himself into an upright position and leaned against the headboard, trying to prepare himself for what she might say in response. If anything. What was worse, the silence or the spoken words? It confused him when she got like that. He found the complex mental mechanisms of women an enigma, a mystery that this one cop would never solve. It was one of the things that drew him in, but he was already regretting having asked, deciding that on this night silence might be safer.

"Trick, I didn't mean to snap at you."

A sigh of relief. "Then what is it?"

"The system. I'm tired. I'm tired of trying to make things better only to be undermined at every turn. I'm tired of kids being returned to parents who don't deserve them. That little boy in the hospital? If he's lucky enough to survive, it's only a matter of time before he's back with the mother that damn near killed him. I hate the system. I hate it Trick"

"But we are the system."

"No, we just work for it. We're nothing more than paid accomplices."

"We promised not to bring our work home," he reminded her. "It's bad for us both."

Ingrid was never one to let emotion overtake logic, but her steeled composure was metamorphosing before his eyes. This case was hitting her hard. He couldn't think of anything to say that wouldn't sound lame.

"We do the best we can with what we've got," he finally said.

"Well isn't that fucking depressing."

In all the time they had been together Trick had never once heard Ingrid swear. And now she was crying. He wrapped his arms around her to comfort her but she pulled away. He held tight and wouldn't let go.

"People shouldn't hurt kids," he said. His voice was soft but filled with gravel and anger.

"Please, just let go of me."

"I'll never let go of you." He ran his fingers through her hair, soft as corn silk, thinking how blessed he was to have found her and how determined he was to keep her. "I love you."

"She's already out," she said.

"Who is?"

"The mother. Child abuse is no more of a crime than a jaywalking ticket."

"From what you've told me she's no flight risk."

"She hasn't got enough for a bus ticket out of town, but that's not the point. Our judge with no judgment made another bad call. I could kill him for giving her one breath of fresh air. She belongs in a cage."

"Sounds like Judge Lambert's been drinking in chambers again. Don't worry. She'll get her day in court."

"That's what worries me, Trick. I have no faith left. I have no faith left in any of it."

She buried her face into his shoulder and sobbed.

"I love you Ingrid," he said, holding her against him. "Please, just don't ever lose your faith in me."

"I love you too."

Her mouth welcomed his kisses and there was a passion and urgency to their love-

making that she rarely saw. His touch was usually gentle and patient, but on occasion it was so wild and untamed that her entire body felt on fire. Tonight was one of those nights and it was what they both needed. It held the anticipation and ecstacy of two teenagers surrendering for the first time in the back seat of a car.

When they'd finished she relaxed into his arms, exhausted. All the tension she'd been feeling had left her and she felt at peace. No words were needed. Their bodies had spoken for them.

There was nothing more to say.

ELEVEN

Big Jim Bullock hung the last of the three Doobie paintings on the living room wall and stood back to admire his handy work. He had to admit they added a much needed splash of color to the surroundings. When they'd returned home from the gallery he was tired, but Paco was running on pure adrenaline and had insisted they drag them in from the car. He wasn't going to be happy until they were hung, never mind that Jim was the one who had to do all the work.

He set the hammer down on the stereo and turned toward Paco where he sat silently in the recliner.

"Well?"

"Well?"

"A thank you would be nice."

"Gracias."

"What the hell are you pouting about? I just spent next year's vacation money on these paintings and if you took one step you'd trip over that bottom lip of yours."

"Why *payaso de rodeo?"* He crossed his arms like a stubborn child.

"What?"

"You told Doobie I was a rodeo clown. You told him I was your cousin. Did you lie because you are ashamed of me?"

"I'm not."

"You are."

"You're nobody's business. And neither am I."

"The big macho *policia* must hide his kindness?"

"Something like that."

"You hurt my feelings."

"Be less sensitive, *Paquito.* Grow some callous over that bronzed, thin skin of yours. I'm sorry, I am, but it's just too damn complicated for you to understand."

"So I am now *estúpido?"*

"No, I don't think you're stupid," he said with an impatient sigh. "It's two o'clock in the morning, Paco. I'm tired."

"This is your *casa* and I am but your guest here. How do you say it in English? You are the one who calls the shots."

"Are you trying to make me feel bad?"

Paco's disposition changed faster than a quarterback zig-zagging toward the end zone. He looked up at Jim and smiled. He leapt up from the chair, forgetting about the cast on his leg and falling forward. Jim caught him before he ended up face first on the floor.

"*Gracias.* The paintings, they are beautiful Chim. You have given me great joy. You have been kind to me and I don't want to make you feel bad. I will be more grateful, I promise."

"Right. Let's just call it a day." What he really wanted to say was don't grovel. It was demeaning, but he didn't want to make Paco feel worse than he already did.

"Yes. Whatever you say Mr. Chim."

"Tomorrow you get that cast removed. That should make you happy."

"Very much so." He hesitated. "And Chim?"

"What now?"

"When the cast is off and I'm all better…will you make me go away?"

"Nobody will ever throw you away again, Paco. I promise."

"And I promise to be no bother."

No bother? Jim looked back at the paintings on the wall. His little stray had already cost him thousands of dollars and a hell of a lot of inconvenience. He'd complicated his life. But he'd also managed to wrap Jim around his little finger.

"My angel," said Paco.

"No, but I'm beginning to think you're mine."

TWELVE

The telephone on the bedside table rang. Big Jim Bullock looked over at the clock. It was three in the morning and he'd been jarred out of a comfortable sleep. There was only one call he'd get at this ungodly hour and he was tempted to let it keep ringing. There were times he wanted to let the old sot end up dead in a ditch. He couldn't remember how he'd ended up being the man's protector. It wasn't a role he enjoyed, not by a long shot. First the Judge and now Paco. That damn soft spot was giving him no end of trouble. He needed to take his own advice to Paco and grow a thicker skin. At least he didn't wear it on his sleeve, unlike his houseguest who flaunted it as though it were something to be proud of. At times Jim found the line between kindness and weakness a blur.

The phone kept ringing.

He reached over and picked up. As he suspected, it was the bartender at the Country Club and the town's Honorable alcoholic had once again tippled himself into a stupor.

"Right," Jim said. "Take his keys and make him stay put. I'm on my way."

At least Paco had some excuse for being helpless. His life had beaten him into submission. Judge Lambert, on the other hand, had no excuse other than weak character combined with a strong lack of judgment. He had no business behind the wheel of a car much less presiding over a courtroom, but Agua Verde was stuck with him until something better came along. And that could be a long time coming.

Jim hung up, dragged himself from the comfort of his bed, threw on some clothes and headed for the door.

It was a dark night made even darker by the lack of street lamps on the residential streets. His headlights were the only light until he turned onto the main drag. He sped toward the edge of town then turned onto the well-manicured grounds of the Agua Verde Country Club. He pulled up in front of the Clubhouse, slammed the car door and headed inside.

Judge Gareth Lambert sat precariously on a bar stool, swaying back and forth as he chatted with the bartender. He was laughing and having a grand old time. Jim couldn't say as much for the bartender.

"You've had enough for tonight," the bartender said, pulling the bottle away from the Judge's outreached hand.

"Awe, c'mon, *jush* one for the road." He broke into song. "*Jush one for my baby and one more for the road*."

"Sorry pal."

"You're no fun. Where's my damn car keys? You steal 'em?" He puffed up his chest and held up his head, stubbled chin pointing toward the ceiling. "May I remind you that theft is a crime?"

"So's drunk driving."

"I can handle it," he said, nearly falling off the bar stool.

Big Jim Bullock walked across the room and placed a hand on Judge Lambert's shoulder. The Judge was wearing his golf clothes, a Polo shirt and gaudy pants, indicating he'd been drinking since before sundown, if not longer.

"It's time to call it a night," he said. The only good thing about Lambert's binges was that he was a damn happy drunk.

The Judge twirled around on the bar stool. "Jim Bullock," he said. "Hey there, *offisher*." He gave Jim an exaggerated salute.

"Let's go," said Jim. "You've had enough happy juice for one night."

"He's had enough to last a week," said the bartender as Jim aimed the Judge towards the exit.

Between his reeling and tripping and insistence of coming to a stop every time he retold a stale joke, steering Judge Lambert to the car was no easy task. It never was. Jim opened the passenger side door and shoved him in. Before he could close it the Judge leaned out, hurling vomit onto the pavement, barely missing Jim's shoes.

"Oops, sorry," the Judge giggled.

"Better the ground than the interior," Jim said with disgust. More than once he'd had to have the car cleaned and deodorized before it was fit to drive again, thanks to the Judge. Your aim is improving, I'll say that for you." He slammed the car door, sidestepped the fresh pool of reeking second-hand drink and bar snacks and slid into the driver's side.

"Home, Jeeves," said the Judge with a wave of his arm.

"I'm fucking tired of playing chauffeur to you and saving your sorry ass."

"Aw, c'mon good buddy," he slurred, sounding like a bad imitation of dialogue from Gilligan's Island.

"I'm not your buddy and this is your last ride home."

His jolly, shit-faced smile turned serious. "You know who I am?"

"The Honorable Judge Gareth Lambert, although I'm hard put to find anything honorable about you."

"I'm important," he said, puffing up his chest.

"Self-important."

"How'm I gonna get home?"

"Next time, walk. I'm not your personal taxi. And don't think I do it because I'm your friend. I do it so somebody doesn't end up dead and I don't want to be the one to clean up the mess." Jim thought for a minute. "Unless..."

"What?"

"I'll make you a deal."

"You gonna start charging me cab fare?"

"If we'd started out that way I'd be a rich man by now. Listen, Agua Verde has a little problem that's causing no end of complaints. Graffiti. It's growing like mold on last month's cheese."

"And one more for the road."

"Try to focus. I've been thinking a lot on it and I've got a solution."

Jim pulled the car to the curb in front of the Judge's house and killed the engine.

The Judge opened his door, leaned over, and puked into the gutter.

"Don't leave yet," he said. "Our talk isn't over. I told you I had an idea."

The Judge slammed the door shut and leaned back in the seat.

"Ban spray paint?" The Judge pulled a handkerchief from his pocket, wiped the spittle from his chin and blew his nose. He shrugged as he shoved it back into his pocket and tried to listen to Jim through his alcohol-induced fog.

"From now on, whenever a gang banger or wannabe punk stands before the bench, whether it's for graffiti or robbery or any other crime, add one little extra to their punishment."

"Like what? I hear it's become unfath-unfashionable to flog them in the town square."

"Oh, this is better. And more constructive. Order them to buy the necessary supplies out of pocket, then send them out to paint over graffiti. Make every damn one of them do it. All over town. And have them wear their orange jump suits, just for humiliation's sake. There's no reason Agua Verde should be paying the bill to clean up their messes."

"Hmmm. It would show the town we're on top of things. I never thought of that."

"Nobody did. And it's so simple. They'll figure out that cleaning it up is harder work than defacing it in the first place. Worth a shot, don't you think?"

The judge sat there, blinking his eyes and trying to form a thought.

"Well?" Jim gave him a nudge. "I'm waiting."

"The grateful citizens of Agua Verde would approve. And I'd get the credit. I'd be as popular as Sheriff Joe Arpaio and we wouldn't even have to dip into the town coffers for pink underwear." The possibilities for self-aggrandizement made him smile. "You've got a deal, good Buddy," said the Judge, one episode too many of Gilligan's Island still swimming in his besotted brain.

"See that you follow through or you can start walking. Better yet, consider retiring that bottle. With all due respect Your Honor, you can't handle it."

But there was no respect due the Honorable Judge Lambert. People weren't blind. And they talked. All Jim could hope for was that the drunken Judge would remember their conversation come morning.

He wondered what reception the Judge received when he entered the house and faced his little trophy wife. His first wife wouldn't have noticed. She was a likeable broad who could drink anyone under the table, including the Honorable Judge. After she'd fallen down the sweeping staircase and broken her neck, there were rumors he might have given her a nudge. The Judge Nudge they called it with snickers. Jim didn't buy that for a minute. Why would he do in his best drinking buddy? There was no motive in his eyes. Drinking was the glue that had held them together.

The Judge's lack of good judgment didn't improve with time or experience.

As for wife number two, Kandi was a piece of work in her own right, having seen the old goat as a step up the social ladder and a way to fill her closets with Valentino and Christian Dior. Pickings were slim for the likes of her and he was one of the few residents of Agua Verde with a big house and a fat wallet who wasn't already taken. And for good reason. No woman in her right mind would consider a happy-go-lucky alcoholic who was the butt of local jokes. Kandi'd been a pole dancer, and heaven knows what else, at one of the local dives and had perfected the use of flattery to acquire big tips and the Judge had fallen for her like a love-struck teenager. The Judge and his new arm candy thought they'd hit the lottery when they'd found each other, but neither one was a prize. Hell, they probably deserved each other.

Jim turned on the car radio to distract himself from thinking of the Judge and his domestic dramas. He dimmed his headlights as he headed back into town. He was tired.

He was tired of graffiti and he was even more tired of being Judge Lambert's free ride home after his frequent benders. Hell, he was just tired. It was the middle of the night and all he wanted was a few more hours sleep.

When he returned home he went to the guest room to check on Paco. He wasn't there.

His heart beat a little louder, a little faster, as he walked from room to room looking for him. When he finally found him he was curled up sound asleep in Jim's bed, his arms wrapped around Jim's pillow.

Jim tiptoed quietly into the room so as not to wake him. He slipped off his shoes, took off his uniform and draped it over a chair, then sat his revolver and his gun belt onto the night stand. He looked down at Paco, sleeping so peacefully with a half-smile on his lips. There was something beautiful about him, like a delicate butterfly.

He gently lifted the covers and slid into the bed beside him.

THIRTEEN

The stench hit them as soon as the manager unlocked the apartment door. The stifling heat didn't help. They weren't met by the smell of rotting flesh, but by the overwhelming aroma of garbage and neglect, feces and decay. At first, Jim Bullock and Trick Delgado didn't see the body. The place was knee-deep in trash and smelled worse than a pig farm during an August heat wave.

"Over there," the apartment manager said, pointing a knobby finger to the floor near the couch. "I didn't see her at first either. How could I with all this mess? It's going to cost big time to get this unit cleaned up. Anyway, like I said, I came banging on her door this morning and she wouldn't open up. I knew she was in there. She always was."

Trick figured the manager for a prime suspect. He had a sneaky aura, like he was hiding something. He had a thin, pointed nose and dark beady eyes that kept darting from side to side to avoid eye contact. "So you found her by accident? Why did you want to speak with her?"

"She was three months behind. When she wouldn't answer I used my key and came in."

Trick took out his notebook, flipped it open and started jotting down notes. "She got a name?"

"Tina. Tina Weston."

"And you?"

"Donnie Crenshaw. Why? All I did was report this."

"It's for our records, Mr. Crenshaw."

Jim looked over at Tina's body, tossed like garbage. Murder was never pretty, but this was plain ugly. The young victim reeked of bad choices. Old take-out cartons and half-eaten food formed a halo around her head as cockroaches danced through her hair, moving the strands as if they were a golden field of wheat being caressed by a soft summer wind. It was ghoulish. Nobody should end up like this. "You were going to evict her?"

"You bet your ass I was. Sorry, but you can ignore just so much. It was get rid of her or have the good tenants give notice. There were too many complaints."

"Do you think one of them killed her?" Big Jim walked through the trash and stood over the body. What a lousy way to start the day. For them both.

"No way. They bitched about the smell and the screaming kid and the scary boyfriend who came and went at all hours. They said cockroaches were coming through the walls. Last thing I want is the expense of having the whole building tented and fumigated. It's not like we have an elite clientele but we do have our standards." Donnie Crenshaw fidgeted with the bottom of his t-shirt, pulling it down, then up, then twisting the hem around his fingers. He looked up at the popcorn ceiling as if it held the answers. "The complaints were nothing serious enough to, you know, kill anybody over." He took a step inside to look at the body again. "I had no idea she'd turned the place into a total shit-hole."

"Why are you so nervous?" asked Jim.

"You shitting me? She's dead, man. I've cleaned up a lot of messes but I never signed on for anything like this." He was tweaking like he'd ingested his breakfast through a well-worn vein. User was tattooed over him from head to toe like a neon sign. But that could wait for another day. Jim and Trick had a fresh corpse to deal with.

"We'll be removing the body, the rest is your problem. Keep out until we're finished."

"You've been a help," said Trick, signaling it was time for the manager to leave. "We'll get back to you if we have more questions."

Donnie adjusted his stained t-shirt then tucked it into jeans that held enough dirt to stand on their own. He wasn't much cleaner than the surroundings. Soap would've been cheaper and done a better job than his cheap aftershave. It didn't mask his body odor. He raised a hand and scratched the stubble on his chin. "One hell of a mess." He shook his head. "From now on I only rent to pensioners. They never cause trouble and they get a Social Security check every month." As an afterthought he added: "And they die of natural causes."

"Thanks again. Now go," said Trick, shaking a cockroach from his foot.

"Right."

"And shut the door."

"Don't go too far," added Jim. "You know the drill?"

"Yeah, in case you have more questions. Like on television. Don't leave town." He snickered, then caught himself.

The door slammed shut and he was gone.

"Jim, you thinking what I'm thinking?" asked Trick.

"What?"

"Why didn't he kick her out a long time ago if she was three months behind on rent? Why wait until the complaints became a problem?"

"It wouldn't be the first time somebody's rent was taken out in trade."

"He'd have to be damn hard up for a lay to set foot in this," he waved his hand around the room, "mess, much less put his dick in..."

"Respect for the dead," Jim reminded his friend.

"Sometimes it's not easy."

They looked down at the body. She was thin, needle marks marched up and down her arms, head tilted to the side at an awkward, unnatural angle.

"You see what I see?"

"You mean *don't* see. There's no blood," said Trick.

"Her neck's been broken by the looks of it."

Trick knelt down next to the body.

"Just like Mrs. Wong," he said.

The door opened and Mackey Hogan stuck in his head.

"Holy crap," he said. "That's the bitch who's kid I took out of here the other night all right. I heard the address over the radio and had to come see for myself. Looks dead as last week's fish and smells even worse." He stifled a gag, closed the door and stepped into the room, landing his shoe in a pile of feces. "Shit." He scraped it off on an exposed section of carpet and put his arm in front of his face, trying to block the odor. "How can people live like this?" Then he laughed. "I guess she couldn't after all. The garbage alone was enough to kill her."

Jim swore that Mackey still had last night's whiskey on his breath. It was hard to tell with all the other smells in the room, but experience told him it was more probable than not. Mackey Hogan drank too much. Sometimes on the job.

"It's a good thing you got that little boy out of here when you did," said Trick. The chill that traveled through his body felt like ice water on burned skin. First Mrs. Wong and now the woman Ingrid told him about who'd abused her kid. It was a small town, but coincidences happened. He disregarded the uneasy feeling deep in his gut, the one that told him there was no such thing as a coincidence, then felt that familiar sensation creeping up the back of his neck and burrowing into his brain. Another migraine collided with his skull. Jagged flickers of light and blind spots played with his vision. He massaged his temples. "It looks like we might have the same killer."

"You're shitting me. A serial killer in Agua Verde?"

"Look."

Mackey knelt down beside the corpse.

"Broken neck. Same m.o." The two cops rose.

"But they're from different worlds," said Trick, reaching into his pocket and pulling out his migraine tablets. He shook out two of them and popped them into his mouth, dry-swallowing them. "It'll be damn hard to make a connection. Mrs. Wong was a business woman. She's just..."

The door flew open. The man standing there looked as bad as the corpse lying on the floor except he was still breathing. He shoved his way into the room. His eyes were as wild as the manager's, like he'd had straight crack for breakfast rather than *snap, crackle, pop*. Jim and Trick pulled their guns and aimed at him.

"This is a crime scene," they said in unison. "Freeze where you are!"

"My baby mama," he said. "Wha' the fuck you do to my baby mama?" He started crying like a kid who'd had his rattle taken away then took an unsteady step forward.

"Freeze," ordered Jim.

The man stopped in his tracks, eyes darting from Mackey to Jim to Trick and back to Mackey. He looked at the guns pointed at him and down at the dead body. "Jesus fucking Christ, whadja do to Tina, dude? She's like dead, man." His eyes landed on Mackey's badge.

"Hogan, Hogan," the guy said, a light bulb going off in his fuzzy brain. "Hogan. She told me all about you. You're the son of a bitch fucking cop who hauled her off and took our kid!"

Pumped on speed and fury, he moved faster than a pickpocket in Grand Central Station, slamming Mackey to the ground before he could react. He had one arm around Mackey's neck while his other hand pulled a switchblade from his pocket, snapped it open and pressed the tip against Mackey's throat, drawing a trickle of blood.

Before he could slice into him, he heard the click and felt the cold steel of Big Jim Bullock's gun pressing against the back of his skull. He dropped the knife and froze.

"My baby mama," he sobbed. "My baby mama. My Tina."

"Face down on the floor!"

The man didn't move.

"Now. Before I pull the trigger."

The man turned and flopped down, landing face-first in the same pile of feces that had dirtied Mackey Hogan's shoe.

"Aw, shit man."

"Hands on top of your head."

He complied.

Trick held him down as Jim pulled his arms around, cuffing his hands behind his back.

Mackey walked over and helped them yank the troublemaker to his feet. He started gagging again at the smell emanating from the guy's face.

"You give the term shit-faced a whole new meaning," he said, retching and laughing at the same time.

"You were a little slow on the uptake," said Trick. "There's some blood on your shirt collar."

"I didn't see it coming."

"That's what makes a cop a dead cop," said Jim, looking into Mackey's bloodshot eyes. "Here," he said, shoving the guy toward him. "Take him down and book him while we finish up here. I'll bet he's got outstanding warrants. Grill the shit out of this guy. Find out who he is and what he's got to do with all this," he said, pointing to the body on the floor.

Mackey Hogan took the man's arm and led him through the door, then turned his head back into the room.

"The meat wagon just pulled up," he said, followed by: "Crap!"

The victim's boyfriend had twisted from Mackey's grip and was running. Mackey followed in pursuit with both Jim and Trick close on his heels. The boyfriend leapt over the railing, apparently forgetting they were on the second floor. The three cops came to a halt, nearly crashing into each other. Trick looked over the railing, the pressure of the blood running to his head and pounding behind his eyes. Below, the man lay in a bed of prickly pear cactus, squirming to free himself, hands still cuffed behind his back as the cactus needles sewed polka dots of beading blood along his pasty skin.

"Need some help down there?" yelled Mackey.

He wiggled some more until he finally rolled off the cactus bed and landed on the pavement next to the stretcher that had arrived to take away Tina Weston. He got to his feet and began to run. One of the men standing by the stretcher extended his leg. He tripped over it and landed face-first onto the pavement, leaving a skid mark of blood red mixed with shit brown.

"Is this our pick-up?" asked the ambulance attendant, smiling up at the three cops.

"Very funny," said Mackey as he headed down the stairs. He cuffed the guy, patted him down for weapons and pulled the wallet from his soiled jeans. Rifling through the wallet, he pulled out a driver's license. The guy continued trying to squirm from Mackey's grip.

"That's the sun up there not a disco ball, so you can stop dancing the brain-dead samba," Mackey said. "We're gonna take a little ride." He looked down at the driver's license again. "Watch your head, Mr. Joey Palermo, we wouldn't want you hurting yourself." Mackey purposely whacked Joey's head against the metal as he shoved him into the squad car, got behind the wheel, and sped away.

"That Hogan's a real piece of work," snorted Trick as he watched from the balcony.

"He could use some fine-tuning," said Jim. "Go back and take more photos before they haul her away. I need to get out of here. Every character in this place is like checking into Hotel Horrible and it makes my skin crawl." He looked at Trick's face. "You okay?"

"Tired, that's all. I didn't get much sleep. You mind writing the report and covering me for a few hours?"

"No problem. I'll meet up with you at headquarters."

"Later then."

"And Jim," Trick said. "Don't forget tonight."

"Tonight?"

"You're still coming over for dinner, right?"

"Is it Saturday already?"

"Go get some rest. It sounds like you need it."

Big Jim Bullock could use a nap, but the first thing on his list was to take Paco to the hospital for his appointment. Poor kid, some of the sympathy he'd been getting would be coming off right along with the cast.

FOURTEEN

Agua Verde, Arizona in summer scorched like a cup of McDonald's java. Heat rose from the pavement like an apparition from hell, shimmered like a thousand rattlesnakes rising from hibernation. Doobie stood on the Main Street sidewalk, portable easel in front of him, brush in hand. He juggled his mixed emotions. On the one hand he was glad that the gallery had been close to a total sell-out of his paintings, on the other hand he was royally pissed that the gallery was demanding more so they could keep the show going to bring in more sales. They both knew that without his one-man shows the place would dry up and die, so he didn't appreciate their treating him like a trained monkey. They needed him a hell of a lot more than he needed them. They knew it and he knew it.

Perspiration burned his eyes. The panhandlers and crazies were already encroaching on his space, sucking up what little oxygen there was in the hot air. They begged or ranted or told him about Jesus. Passers-by paused to watch him paint—buildings, cars, busses, the trolley to nowhere—assuming he was just one more starving artist. Some offered an insulting ten or twenty bucks. His responses fell short of polite. "Not for sale. Fuck off," he'd say, dismissing them with a wave of his hand. Doobie wasn't starving. He wasn't even hungry. His watercolors topped the thousand dollar mark and his shows sold out. He loved to paint. He loved his cats. He loved his pot and his Japanese sake. He viewed people with contempt. Yoriko was the sole exception. Doobie was pushing seventy. Yoriko was barely legal with the body of a twelve year old. She was his lover and his latest muse.

The heat was causing the paint to dry before it hit the paper. He rose, frustrated, focused his digital camera, clicked off ten shots before packing it in. One good shot of the trolley, a car passing on the left, ass end of a bus heading south. That one had possibilities. He should have enough fodder for the following Friday's show. Painting outdoors was crazy in this heat and impossible during monsoon season, so he'd shoot photos and paint in the air conditioned comfort of his home studio. Today was becoming one of those days. A bit of a cheat but it got the job done.

Doobie shoved the supplies into the back seat of his car then settled in behind the wheel. Traffic pulled over to the side as a cop car flew past, blasting its shrill siren. He waited impatiently. Agua Verde was turning from calm to chaos. What had once been an unnoticed desert oasis was changing before his eyes. Too much traffic, noise, crime—too many people. Not as crowded as Phoenix or Tucson, not by a long shot. Certainly not as crowded as the San Francisco he'd left behind, but not good either. He'd always missed the early days in SF. He'd been a major player during the beatnik heyday of drugs, jazz, group sex, literature, Lawrence Ferlinghetti poetry, and meaningful art. It had been a feast for the senses back then. Inspirationally cool, man. Before the hippies descended on the Haight. They were the pretenders. The beats had been the real thing.

His mind wandered as he pulled into traffic and drove home.

There were days he missed San Francisco, even thought of returning. But the place he had loved didn't exist anymore. It was yesterday's news lost in time. He knew that seeing it now would damn near break his heart.

So Agua Verde it was.

* * * *

That afternoon the ragtag group of cops gathered in the conference room. Big Jim Bullock fed the tape from Jia Wong's store into the hungry mouth of the player. He sat down next to Trick Delgado then hit the play button. The image was fuzzy, then cleared to reveal the empty store from where the recorder had been placed high, above and behind the cash register.

"Nothing," said one of the cops.

"Shut up and watch," said Chief Irwin. "There might be something on here that we can use."

"What am I even here for?" asked Mackey Hogan. "I should be working on this morning's jewelry store robbery."

"That can wait. Murder trumps robbery."

No sooner had he spoken than the tape came to life. A man entered the store, followed by two others. The three of them were dressed in low-slung pants like big city gang-bangers with strides to match. They looked around the room. No one was standing behind the register. One of them spoke to his friends, but the film had no audio. The three of them gave the room one more look, then two of them went to the refrigerator case and pulled out a couple twelve packs. Static and lines filled the screen and it went black.

"Damn it," said the Chief.

The screen stayed black for a good three minutes as the cops sat impatiently in their chairs.

"That wasn't much help," William Washington said. "Our job would be easier if people would update their surveillance cameras. This is as bad as watching an old Beta."

The screen flickered and came to life again. The top of a head filled the screen, then appeared full-figure, the man's arms filled with cartons of cigarettes. He reached over to the cash register then looked down, lips moving as he motioned to his friends.

"Freeze frame that," said the Chief.

"Check out those two goof balls in the background," said Mackey Hogan. "What's that old geezer doing with those other two. Damn, his hair is white as rice and look at his skin…"

"White as his hair," said Trick. "Doesn't look like he's spent a day in the sun. Probably not a local by the looks of him."

The third accomplice stood in perfect profile. "Check out that schnozzola!" Mackey laughed. "We can put out an APB for the guy with the biggest nose in town and probably have him in ten minutes. A person can hide a lot, but that snot-locker stands out like an Alabama Porch Monkey at a KKK picnic."

William Washington clenched his black fist but said nothing.

"You could use some sensitivity training," said Big Jim to Mackey. "And you could use a few lessons in the King's English."

"So I'm not politically correct," Mackey shrugged. "So what?" Then as an afterthought he turned to William Washington: "No offense meant, *Willie*."

Washington bristled but remained silent.

Their attention returned to the tape.

The three murder suspects ran out of the store, arms filled with their booty of free beer and cigarettes.

"The guy closest to the camera," said Trick. "I recognize him. I've pulled him in more than once on possession."

"His name?" asked Chief Irwin.

"Let me think." Trick racked his brain trying to bring up the name. "I can't remember."

"Remember, Delgado. Then get an address and haul him in," the Chief said. "And take Bullock with you. It looks like we might just have our killer."

The men rose. William Washington walked up to Mackey Hogan and stood just a bit too close. Mackey took a step backwards, giving Washington just the space he needed to punch his fist into Mackey's face. Mackey let out a grunt as he fell to the floor, holding his nose as he tried to stop the flow of blood.

"A guy can take just so much," said William with a shrug.

Mackey rose to his feet, fury in his eyes as he looked around the room at the other officers. "You saw it. The son-of-a-bitch attacked me. That's assault." Then to Washington: "You're going down for this."

"What are you talking about?" asked the Chief. "Nobody hit you. You tripped over that chair and fell face first onto the floor."

"That's what I saw," said Jim Bullock.

"Me too," said Trick.

One by one the officers agreed that they'd witnessed nothing but Mackey's nosedive to the squad room floor.

"I can't believe you guys won't back me up on this."

"You'd better get that nose looked at," said the Chief. "It looks broken. And have the paramedics wash your mouth out with soap while they're at it."

"You've got to be shitting me…Sir."

"Consider yourself on temporary medical leave. And if you don't clean up your act and your mouth, you're out of here. Permanently." He looked over at Washington and smiled. "William, can you work on the jewelry store robbery as well as help out on Jia Wong's murder?"

"Yes, sir. Thank you sir."

"Good. Now everyone get out of here and get to work. You're dismissed."

The Chief picked up the ringing phone. "What? Crap, that's all we need," he said to the voice at the other end. "Hold up," he yelled, stopping the cops before they reached the door. He slammed down the receiver.

"Mackey."

"Yes, sir?" he said, blood still trickling from his broken nose.

"That crack-head you booked earlier. They just found him hanging in his cell."

"No loss," Mackey shrugged.

"It puts us in a world of shit."

"Not my problem. Sir. I'm on medical leave." He wiped the blood from under his nose. "It's not like anybody's going to miss the guy." He turned and walked out the door.

Trick Delgado remained silent. Fate had managed to kill two birds with one stone. Ingrid wouldn't have to worry about that little kid being returned to either parent. They'd be sharing a slab in the morgue.

"I guess that solves the case," said Trick. "He killed his baby-mama then he killed himself. Case closed."

"Not so fast," said the Chief.

"What, you've got at least one case tied up in a neat little ribbon. No reason to complicate something simple."

"Maybe too neat."

The Chief wasn't one to take anything at face value. Sure, it might be simple. He might have hanged himself. Sure, it might look like it was a suicide, but the rising body count certainly deserved some speculation on his part. It was his job to scrutinize all the angles. It was bad police work to zero in on the easiest answer without looking outward to all other possibilities. That neat little ribbon might be just that, but it could just as well unravel like a cheap sweater.

FIFTEEN

Saturday night crept up like a snake on a quail and caught Jim Bullock by surprise. He had stopped at the market and picked up the ingredients to make the special cheesecake he'd promised Trick he'd bring for their dinner. And a twelve-pack. He'd probably need to drink half of it to get through another of Ingrid's fix-ups. If Trick weren't his best friend he'd tell her to knock off the blind dates. They were torture. She couldn't resist parading her female friends past him one at a time despite the fact he was yet to meet one with whom he clicked. Tonight promised to be nothing more than another chapter in her never-ending ritual.

But Trick and Ingrid were his friends so he'd shut his mouth and make the best of it.

Paco watched as Jim worked in the kitchen. He was doing his kicked puppy routine again, not understanding why his angel insisted on keeping him under wraps. Jim tried to explain, then tried to appease him by making an extra cheesecake just for him. It was a lame effort at best.

"Cheesecake, Mr. Chim? This does not look like cheese and it does not look like cake."

Jim slid the blueberry cheesecake across the counter and handed Paco a fork. "Take a bite."

Cautiously, Paco lifted the fork to his mouth. He waited for the first bite to melt in his mouth before swallowing. A big smile washed across blueberry stained teeth. His second bite was larger than the first. "Good," he said. "This is all for me?"

"Have at it." Jim covered the second cheesecake with plastic wrap and slide it into a brown grocery bag, then removed the twelve pack from the fridge. "Gotta go now. Don't open the door to anyone and don't pick up the phone if it rings. I'll probably be home early."

Paco walked around the counter and up to Jim and gave him a hug.

"Early would be nice."

Jim walked out the door, hands full and head prepared to face another night of the Ingrid's matchmaking and Trick's good company. They could leave the murders in the office and relax as if the world were a better place.

It wasn't and they both knew it, but an evening of drinking and pretending would feel damn good.

* * * *

The four of them sat on the patio and watched the sun sink like a donut in a cup of hot coffee. Once it dropped below the horizon the bats began their nightly swoop, grabbing insects as they zig-zagged across the darkening sky and over the mesquite trees and tall cacti. The quartet watched lazily, their stomachs full and their beer cold, laughing as the bats swooped down and scooped up water from the swimming pool with their tongues.

Ingrid hadn't been kidding; his blind date was a knockout. Jennifer was a cute little brunette with a pouty Gloria Grahame mouth and a body to match. Her conversation was clever and flirtatious and her laughter was like bubbles in a glass of expensive champagne. She wore pale pink lipstick and a matching dress that clung to her body in all the right places. He hated to admit it, but she was good company. Ingrid caught his eye and smiled. He gave her a subtle wink and took a long draw from his sweating beer bottle. If the two women were setting a trap they were doing a damn good job of it. Things could be worse. They small-talked and laughed as though three dead bodies with broken necks weren't asleep in the morgue.

"What do you do?" he asked Jennifer, in an awkward attempt to move their conversation forward.

"I own Fashionista. The little boutique on Main Street," she replied. "Pretty boring stuff compared to being a police officer."

"I doubt that, but boring definitely has its rewards."

"That's hard to believe."

"Being a cop fluctuates from uneventful to adrenaline-pumping excitement with lots of dead air in between. The problem with the exciting part is that it's always mixed in with tragedy or ruined lives. It's sad."

"You don't sound like a cop. I thought you guys got off on the action."

"Some do."

"Being a cop isn't that different from being a criminal," said Ingrid. "It's like the flip side of the same coin. It's like those old black and white movies where one brother becomes a cop and the other becomes a gangster. When you peel away the layers they aren't so different. They both use guns, they just use them to different ends."

"The psychiatrist speaks," said Trick.

"It's true. They both live by the gun. And sometimes die by it."

"That's a bit dramatic."

"Forgive my honesty."

The unspoken tension between them didn't escape Jim. Trouble in paradise? It wasn't easy being married to a cop, but Ingrid always handled it fine. Something was bothering her. He took another sip of his beer. Jennifer leaned over to talk with Ingrid, who had been rather quiet all evening, except for the occasional barb. He could tell by Trick's expression that he was as puzzled as himself.

He heard Jennifer whisper to Ingrid: "He reminds me of Tom Selleck," to which she replied: "A much younger one, I hope."

"1980's Selleck. The one with the sexy moustache."

They giggled.

Trick and Ingrid had been right. A night like this was just what they needed.

Jennifer leaned back and stretched, her foot not so subtly rubbing against his calf. She waited for a reaction but he didn't make eye contact, just stared off into the night sky. Slightly embarrassed, she switched gears.

"Agua Verde's changing," she said. "I was born and raised here. I used to think it was dull, but when I grew up I liked it because it was quiet. Lately though..."

"When populations grow so does the crime rate," said Trick. "It's the same everywhere."

"But two murders? And so close together?"

"And don't forget the supposed suicide," said Ingrid.

"What do you mean supposed?" asked Trick.

"Three broken necks? What are the odds? You're the one who always says there's no such thing as a coincidence."

Trick shrugged but remained silent.

"Suicide?" They happen everywhere," said Jennifer.

"Not in a jail cell," said Ingrid. "Not in Agua Verde anyway."

Trick and Jim exchanged glances.

"Suicide," said Jim, almost to himself. "A permanent solution to a temporary problem."

"It never should've happened," said Trick. "Mackey Hogan booked him and must've forgotten to remove the guys belt before putting him in the cell."

"Mackey was a little quick to nail Tina Weston's murder on the guy. The captain, he's not so sure." Jim shrugged and took a slug of his beer. "Me? I'm not so sure either."

Jennifer looked into Jim's eyes. "That jewelry store that was robbed is just a few doors down from Fashionista. I don't feel safe anymore."

"You've got two of the best cops in town right here," said Ingrid. "Not to worry. Now, no more shop talk, okay? That's the rule but we've backslid right into it. Let's change the subject to something happier."

The two men rose and headed for the kitchen.

"It looks like you two hit it off," said Trick.

"She's nice."

"That'll please Ingrid no end."

"It's none of my business, but what's up with her? She's tossing barbs at you like ninja stars. That's not like her."

"Something's eating at her. Maybe the job. I don't know. She keeps things bottled up."

Jim reached for another beer.

"She's no different than the rest of us," said Trick. "Everybody carries around a big shovel looking for whatever it is that will fill that empty hole they carry inside. I was hoping she could fill hers with me."

"C'mon Trick, you two are perfect together. Don't borrow trouble where there isn't any."

"You're right. It's probably nothing but work stress."

"And a cop's wife always worries if he's going to make it home."

The two men walked back out onto the patio and sat down.

They talked and drank until the four of them had achieved a pleasant buzz, then rose and went back into the welcome coolness of the house. The temperatures at night weren't much cooler than daytime and air conditioners chugged away around the clock, utility bills be damned. Even a native desert rat could take just so much. On the upside, when it reached the triple digits, the crime rate usually went down. This week had been the exception. Three dead bodies and not one spent bullet. Usually pulling the tab-top on a can was about all the locals could muster until things cooled down. They swore they could feel autumn in the air when the thermometer dipped to a bearable ninety-eight.

"Benji!" Trick yelled, making them jump. "The guys name is Benji."

"What guy?" asked Ingrid.

"The one on the tape. The one that robbed and killed Jia Wong. His name was Benji. Benji something or other. I can't remember his last name."

"It'll come to you. We'll take another look at the tape in the morning," said Jim. "It might jog something."

"Tomorrow's Sunday, for God's sake. Can't you two ever relax?"

"Just for a few hours." Trick leaned over and kissed Ingrid's cheek. "I promise."

"Fine. Maybe I'll go visit your mother."

"What on earth for?"

"She's the only in-law I've got. Who knows? Maybe I'll find her in a good mood."

"She doesn't have a good mood."

The four of them stood awkwardly around the kitchen island, none of them wanting to be the first to suggest calling it a night. Trick washed down a migraine pill with his beer, raised his bottle and clanked it against the other three. "Here's to good friends and good times," he said with a slight slur, draining the bottle's contents. "Anybody ready for another?"

Ingrid got the signal. "I think we've had enough. Jim has to drive." She looked over at him. Her smile told him she was pleased that he and Jennifer hit it off. "You're the most sober one here, Jim. Would you mind dropping Jennifer home? I think Trick's had one too many."

Step two of the trap, he thought.

"I can walk, really. I live above the boutique. It's only a few minutes away."

"We'll have none of that." They said their goodnights and Jim and Jennifer headed for the door.

Trick turned to Ingrid. "You're still tense. I'd have thought you'd be happy knowing that little boy won't go back to his parents."

"I'm glad they're dead." She edged closer to her husband and kissed his cheek. They stood in the doorway and watched as Jim and Jennifer drove away.

* * * *

Taking Jennifer home was a quick drive. They pulled up to the curb. Jim looked down the street, to the flickering neon of Flaming June's. It seemed like only yesterday he'd rescued Paco from his assailants right along this very sidewalk. And it seemed a lifetime ago.

"Would you like to come up for a cup of coffee?"

They both knew that coffee didn't mean coffee.

"I'm really tired. I hope you don't mind if I take a rain check."

"Next time then," she said, trying to hide her disappointment. She leaned across the seat and kissed him, putting her all into it. It was a surprisingly hungry kiss from such soft lips. Jim kissed her back. No sparks. No fireworks. No fire. No smoke anywhere but in her eyes. No arousal, at least not on his part. He wondered if she sensed that he felt nothing at all.

He tried to fake it but he might just as well have been kissing his maiden aunt.

"You'd better get upstairs before I change my mind," he lied, relieved when she finally exited the car. He watched as she headed for the side stairs that led to her apartment above the boutique. She paused, then turned and waved.

He'd survived the evening. A few minutes later he pulled into his driveway, then through the front door.

"I'm home," he called.

"Señor Chim!" came an excited voice from the other end of the house.

SIXTEEN

Sunlight dove through the window, promising another sizzling day. Doobie the artist and his girlfriend Yoriko sat in silence as they sipped their morning tea. They shared a joint as she read the Sunday morning paper, passing the fat cigarette back and forth between hits, the pungent scent of marijuana filling the room. He never read the paper, had no interest in the outside world or its problems. Painting and Yoriko were enough to fill his universe. He watched as she sat across from him in her red silk embroidered kimono. She turned the page of the newspaper and the silken sash fell loose, exposing one tiny breast. The sight of her sepia nipple, kissed by the morning sun, aroused him. This morning everything about her aroused him, from her perfect little girl body to her pink mouth that puckered like a lotus bud not yet in full blossom. Her very presence was more potent than Viagra and twice as effective. When he was with her he felt like twenty again and acted accordingly.

When he stood up she didn't seem to notice that he'd sprouted a full-blown erection.

"A drive-by on the south side, Doobie," she said aloud as she read. "A jewelry store robbed yesterday on Main Street. A van full of illegals crashed north of Tubac."

"Forget that crap," he said, pulling her from her chair and leading her into the bedroom. Their sex always got his artistic juices flowing. The vase of peacock feathers on the night stand were more than decorative and his imagination on the mattress was matched only by his creativity with brush and paint. That, not to mention his money and an address considered elite by Agua Verde standards, made him damn attractive to a young, nubile chick.

Life was good.

SEVENTEEN

The Agua Verde police station was empty except for Trick Delgado and his best friend, Big Jim Bullock. After reviewing the tape from Jia Wong's store one more time, Trick ejected it from the player and slid it back into its box. "What a crappy way to spend Sunday morning. But it beats the hell out of sleeping it away on a hard church pew. Which reminds me, where did you end up sleeping last night?" He gave Jim a wink.

"In my bed."

"Could'a fooled me the way the electricity was flying."

"You can tell Ingrid she hit a home run. Jennifer's a real cutey. But I don't want to rush things."

"Rush things? The entire male population would kill for what you've got and you're letting it go to waste. Women get a sniff of that testosterone level and trip over each other just trying to get to you. Jesus Christ, man, don't you ever need to get laid?"

Jim said nothing.

"Okay, I get it. It's none of my business, but as your friend I have to say that living the life of a monk isn't healthy. Sometimes it's good to let loose. It sure as hell relieves my tension after a day in this shit hole."

Jim wondered if Trick knew the truth. The two of them were best friends but even friends have their secrets. Everyone has a secret or two they keep locked inside. Some things just aren't anyone else's business.

Jim shrugged his muscular shoulders and changed the subject.

"With your background in Special Forces you could've been hired anywhere. Maybe even the Secret Service for God's sake. You were a hero. Why here?"

"Hero's an over-used word. Hell, even I don't remember half of it. I guess because they make you do shit over there that's best forgotten."

Jim nodded in agreement. Although he'd never been a soldier himself, he could well imagine the horrors of war. "But why here?" he asked again.

"Because Agua Verde is home."

They returned to their desks.

"About the sex thing..." said Trick, awkwardly moving the subject from his military background. It was a chapter of his life kept buried beneath a tombstone that was too heavy to lift.

"What woman wants to put all her chips on a guy who *might* make it home at night?" Jim said. "We're not perfect husband material."

"Are you from an Amish farm or a closet Mormon or something?" asked Trick. "Crap, a one night stand beats waiting for perfection. If you wait for your ideal you'll be too old to get it up."

"Point taken."

"Just saying." Trick dismissed a thought that had passed through his mind more than once.

"We need to track down this Benji guy. Anything jog your memory yet?"

Trick got the hint. Change the subject. He took a long sip of coffee from his Styrofoam cup and wrinkled his nose. "I miss Jia Wong's coffee. I can't find another one that measures up.

This stuff from Candy's tastes almost as bad as the crap I get at home." He sat the cup down on a pile of forgotten paperwork. "Benji. Benji *B-something.* It's right on the tip of my tongue. Bor, Bor, Bor something. Bordain. Benjamin Bordain. That's it!"

"Bordain. Sounds like a bad French wine."

"He was like a pound of hamburger you forgot in the trunk of your hot car. You could smell the guy from across the room."

Trick booted up the computer and clicked. "Let's see this guys history." He clicked and scrolled and entered the name. Benjamin Bordain's rap sheet popped up. Benji. It was a long one, but far from impressive. "Nothing but crap crimes. Possession or an occasional barroom assault or petty theft. "I remember him now. The guy was born trouble and weaned on idiot pills. Raised by a mom who couldn't rein him in. He'd sit in jail for a few months then head right back to mama."

"Hardly seems like the murdering type," said Jim.

"None of 'em do until it's done."

"It doesn't look like he has that much ambition. But that was definitely him on the tape from Jia Wong's. Maybe he escalated."

"Killing for a six-pack and some smokes. Yeah, he's definitely dumb enough."

"Any idea where he might be now?"

"Mama never had what it took to kick out his sorry ass."

"Ah, motherly love," said Jim.

"Some got it and some don't." Peggy Delgado sure as hell doesn't, he thought. Even when he'd returned from the service a hero she'd wasted no time bursting his bubble. "Let's take a drive. I'd bet he's still glued there like a fly on horse shit."

The door opened and Chief Irwin entered the room.

"What're you two doing here?" He asked. "Isn't this your off day?"

"We had an itch to scratch," said Jim. "This Jia Liu case is enough to give a person insomnia."

The Chief gave Trick Delgado a sideways glance and retreated to his office.

"You see that?" asked Trick.

"What? His bad comb-over?"

"The way he looked at me. I don't like the way he looked at me."

"He probably thinks you're crazy for working on your day off."

"Let's get out of here."

The two men rose and walked out the door into the hot Agua Verde sun. "You drive," Trick said, shielding his eyes from the glare, a sure-fire migraine trigger. That was the last thing he needed today.

They had a scumbag to collar and murders to solve.

EIGHTEEN

The house was no larger than a shipping box, hastily erected back in the late 1940's to house the returning soldiers from World War II. The stucco siding peeled like a bad sunburn and the window frames showed years of rot from the scorching desert sun. Weeds stretched their fingers through the cracks in the walkway that led to the front door. Trick looked around at the front yard. Creosote plants had reproduced with no birth control until the yard looked like a gnarled jungle. A dying cactus lay among the creosote, its brown and wrinkled corpse gasping for a drop of water.

"If the guy's still mooching off mama, the least he could do is work the yard," said Trick. "Disgusting."

They walked up to the front door and Big Jim knocked, scraping a knuckle on the peeling paint. He licked a drop of blood off his hand and knocked again.

Finally the door opened a crack to expose sad blue eyes behind the lens of 1950's cat eye glasses. "Yes?" she asked with a cautious whisper.

"Mrs. Bordain?"

She nodded, opening the door a few more inches.

"Do you mind if we ask you a few questions?" asked Big Jim as he flashed his badge.

"What did Benji do now?" She sighed, opened the door wide, and motioned them in. None of what they saw was what they'd expected. The interior of the house was obsessive/compulsive neat and spotless and rather than looking like the mother of a troublemaker they usually saw, she actually looked sweet, with a face as cute as a Pekingese puppy despite the worry wrinkles around her eyes. Her blind mother's love and gentle demeanor had made her Benji's doormat.

Mrs. Bordain nodded towards the sofa, welcomed them to sit, then offered them lemonade, which they politely declined. Their reason for being there was hardly cause for her hospitality, but the weary woman had been there before and accepted their presence with unusual and unexpected grace. She sat in an antique brocaded chair across from them. On the coffee table between them was a photograph. In the picture a young mother looked lovingly down at her little boy, the man who must have been the father was glancing down at his young son who already had a spark of mischief in his eyes.

Mrs. Bordain noticed them glancing at the photo. "That is…was," she corrected herself, "my husband Jack. He was a good man, Chief Engineer in the Merchant Marines. The asbestos got him years ago. If God hadn't taken him things with Benji might have turned out differently." The sadness in her eyes deepened. "Why are you here?"

"We just want to ask him a few questions," said Jim. "Is he home?"

"I'm not sure."

How could she not be sure? She saw the question on their faces. "No, I'm not hiding anything," she said in her soft voice. "After the last time he got out of jail I just didn't have the heart to kick him out. Where would he go? I had him set up a living space out in the garage so I wouldn't have to see his comings and goings. He's probably out there, but I can't say for sure."

"Would you mind?" asked Trick.

Mrs. Bordain stood and motioned them to follow her. The three of them walked through the pink tiled kitchen that led to the back door. She pointed to the garage. "He comes in and out from that side door," she said as she retreated back into the house.

* * * *

There was no response when Big Jim Bullock knocked on the garage door. They waited a few more minutes, knocked a few more times, then Trick Delgado jiggled the door knob. It was unlocked. The door squeaked on rusty hinges as they entered, the only light dimly entering the space through a small, dusty and cobwebbed window. Benji Bordain wasn't there. Where there should have been a car in the small, one car garage sat a beat up sofa and an old wooden crate that served as a table. Unlike the inside of the main house, the small table held empty beer bottles and an ashtray filled with stale cigarette butts. An old ladder leaned against a high storage shelf where a mattress lay, an old quilt lay across the bed and draped over the top of the ladder.

"Cool digs," said Trick with a snort. "Might as well come back tomorrow and try to catch him home then. It's Sunday and I want to get home to Ingrid anyway."

"Suits me fine."

The two cops exited the side door and headed to the car.

Big Jim Bullock had someone to go home to as well.

NINETEEN

Kandi lay in the king size bed and pulled up the goose down comforter to cover her naked body. Early Monday morning sunlight flashed across the bedroom screaming of another hot day in Agua Verde. Judge Lambert stood in front of the full length mirror, wrestling with his boxer shorts and wheezing. She was anxious for him to leave so that she could wash his filth off her body. Sex with him, if you could call it sex, was like lying underneath a huge, greasy balloon that reeked of yesterday's stale whiskey. The judge struggled to get the boxers over his large stomach, a stomach that hung so low that it nearly covered his penis. If his pathetic dick had been any smaller he'd have been a woman and a damn ugly one at that. She looked around the room, filled with brocades, silks, crystal chandeliers and opulence. Neither of them had a clue as to what was actually good taste. The decor was more like east coast Mafia or 1970's Liberace, gaudy and over the top rather than subtle. She hated pretending she actually cared for him but it was a small price to pay for her luxurious lifestyle and a wallet full of shopping money.

There was a time in her life when she'd done a lot more for a lot less.

Kandi knew her body was her greatest asset and she'd learned early on just how to use it. Dear Uncle Charlie had been playing with her body before she had even reached puberty and always brought her little presents. A doll, a candy bar, whatever. He was always happy to babysit his little niece in that ramshackle trailer in the middle of nowhere. She'd told her mother what they'd been doing and either she didn't believe her or didn't care or maybe it was just a normal thing that all little girls and their uncles did. All her mother really cared about was getting her next fix and if she didn't have the cash she'd look the other way as strangers took Kandi into the other room. That was the reality of her childhood and with no life to compare it to, she had no sense of what might be right or wrong. By the time she reached fourteen she'd left home and started turning tricks. She saw it as an opportunity rather than a start down a dangerous road but at sixteen she'd lied about her age and got a job as an exotic dancer, a step up the ladder from the streets. Men tripped over each other to get near her and the night she caught Judge Gareth Lambert's eye it opened the door to a new life. She flirted, taunted him with her gyrations, told him lies. Giving him lap dances was like bouncing on an overstuffed pillow but her body had served her well.

She watched as he pulled on his pants and buttoned his shirt. No matter how well he dressed it couldn't hide what an obnoxious man he was. His ego was as inflated as his body but she fed it and flattered it at every turn. She'd wrapped the fool around her finger, the finger that toyed with her wedding band and a three carat diamond ring.

The old fart had been an easy catch.

Judge Lambert fumbled with his tie and finally knotted it with fingers the size of Polish sausages. He turned to her with a smug grin, waiting for his compliment.

"You look very distinguished," Kandi said with a smile. "I'm a lucky woman."

Last night she'd checked his court calendar and today was empty. She'd resigned herself to him being with her all day and spoiling her plans, but here he was dressed and ready to leave. He'd likely spend the day on a barstool at the Country Club, drinking his breakfast, lunch and dinner. The day would be hers and she knew just how to fill it.

The rumble of a gas lawn mower starting up filled the bedroom. Gareth tipped his head and listened, nodding approval. He turned to Kandi. "Tell that guy when he's done mowing to check the chlorine level in the swimming pool and fish out the leaves, okay?"

"He has a name, Gareth. I think it's Cal something."

"Cal, Hal, Sal, what's the difference? He's hired help and I don't really give a flying rat's ass if he has a name or not. Just hand him his check when he's finished."

Oh, how she enjoyed having access to that checkbook.

So be it. Cal was the best hired help they'd had. He maintained the grounds and the pool, took orders and did a good job. Just looking through the window watching him work shirtless stirred something deep inside of her. And Cal also cared for Kandi's needs. He serviced her well and was a wonderful lover. Stupid Gareth was none the wiser and Cal filled her every craving. He was young, buff and virile. Just what the doctor ordered. Sex had never meant anything to her before. It was just an act, a tool to get what she wanted. But when Cal embraced her it awakened feelings and sensations she had never felt before. He'd given her the first orgasm she'd ever experienced and something inside of her blossomed that had been dead her entire life. Whether it was love or lust didn't matter. All that mattered was that it felt damn good.

He was her addiction as much as her mother's heroin had been hers.

She smiled at her husband as he turned and left the room. She waited until she heard the car door slam and the purr of his engine starting up, then threw off the comforter and headed for the shower.

Kandi had the best of both worlds.

TWENTY

The squad room filled up early. Chief Irwin stood stiff shouldered and looked around the room. The cops were all there, save one. Big Jim Bullock sat next to his friend Trick Delgado, and William Washington leaned back and relaxed as well as one could in the wobbly wood chair. The absence of Mackey Hogan certainly lent a more relaxed atmosphere to their surroundings. He hoped that putting the son-of-a-bitch on temporary medical leave would teach him a lesson, like learning when to keep his mouth shut. If there had been a replacement he would have shit-canned him long ago but there was never an overload of applications of cops hungry to work in a nowhere town with little action and measly pay.

Chief Irwin made due the best he could with what he had. After that incident had caught up with him back in Jersey he'd ended up here himself, the place where cops went when there was nowhere else to go. It had been a stupid mistake, what he'd done, but half the department had been on the take back then. He'd just been the unfortunate one who had been caught. And they'd only known the half of it. But he felt he was a good cop when all was said and done. At least here he'd earned a higher rank. The bigger fish in the smaller pond so to say, although the pond was more of a mud puddle.

Bullock, Delgado and Washington were all good cops and did their jobs well. He could hardly say the same for Hogan. Chief Irwin would have been better off hiring a trained monkey.

"William Washington," he said. "Have you made any progress on the jewelry store robbery?"

"I've talked with the owner, as well as the customers who were in the store at the time,

but so far no one has recognized the guy. I have a vague description, greasy and shifty looking, not much to go on but I doubt he was a local. I'll keep working on it sir."

"Bullock, Delgado. Any breaks on the Jia Wong murder?"

Trick Delgado spoke up. "I've identified one of the three that were in the store video. A small time hoodlum named Benjamin Bordain. I checked his rap sheet and he's normally just small potatoes but maybe he's escalated."

"We went to his address to bring him in for questioning, but he wasn't there," said Jim. "We're going to head back there today. At least we know where he hangs his hat."

"Solving this one is top priority, Bullock. And William, keep up the good work on the robbery. I want a better report on both of these by tomorrow so step it up." Chief Irwin gave a wave of dismissal. The sound of wood chairs scraping against wood floors accompanied them as they rose and left the room to face another day.

"I'm glad the Chief got Mackey Hogan out of our hair," said Trick to William Washington. "Nobody should have to put up with his shit."

"It's definitely more pleasant," said William, a man who carefully chose his words. "I'm not fond of the man."

"None of us are," said Big Jim.

"I'll see you two later," said William Washington as he headed in the opposite direction to his car, carrying himself with dignity and resolve.

"William is one cool character. I couldn't hold myself together like he does," said Trick. "Not with all the insults Mackey's tossed his way."

"He's kind of a mystery man, keeping to himself the way he does," said Jim. "We really don't know anything about him. Not the man behind the badge, anyway." Jim shoved his hands in his pockets and changed the subject. "Cup of Joe at Bad Sandy's before we head out?"

"Sounds like a plan. And Jim…"

"Yeah?"

"I apologize for the other day. I didn't mean to nose into your private business."

"No harm, no foul."

* * * *

Big Jim and Trick headed up the walkway to the front door of Mrs. Bordain's house. She'd been so cooperative when they'd last spoken with her that they wanted to extend the courtesy of letting her know that they were heading back to talk with her wayward son Benji.

Jim knocked and when she opened the door they were met with her sweet, tired smile.

"Would you like to come in?" she offered, resigned to their presence. There was a fragility about her, so no reason to tell her that her son was the prime suspect in the murder of Jia Wong, just that they wanted to ask him a few questions. She pointed them in the direction of the garage. "I think I heard him go in late last night" she volunteered, glad they were going to him from the side of the house rather than marching through her kitchen again. She'd reached the point of wanting to distance herself as far as she could from her son's problems. She had already done the best she could and had accepted her failure. She still loved Benji, he was her only child, but she wasn't blind to his lack of character.

She'd lost the battle to save him long ago.

Trick knocked on the side door of the garage. There was no response so he knocked again with one of those loud cop bang, bang, bangs that could wake the dead. Still no response.

Impatiently, he jiggled the knob and the door opened. The two men entered, adjusting their eyes to the darkness. The number of beer bottles on the table had multiplied like horny rabbits since their last visit and the place reeked of stale cigarette smoke and a hint of urine.

Jim glanced around the room and spotted the bundle of clothes lying on the floor near the ladder that led to the small sleeping shelf. As he walked over to take a closer look he saw that the under the bundle of clothes lay the body of Benjamin Bordain. At first he thought the kid was sleeping off a bender but when he knelt down and felt the pulse in his neck, there was no doubt that Benji was cold and very dead.

There was no blood. But his neck appeared to be broken.

"Holy crap," said Trick as he knelt beside him.

"I don't think he'll be talking with us any time soon."

Trick looked up at the ladder that was leaning askew against the high storage shelf. "Looks like the stupid drunk went ass over appetite trying to climb the ladder," he said. "Damn."

Jim pulled the rubber gloves from his pocket and put two of the beer cans in an evidence bag. "With a little work we can run the numbers on the cans to verify if that beer came from Wong's."

"At least that would prove we're on the right track."

"Do you want the good job or the bad job?" Jim asked him, dreading the answer.

"I'll take care of the calls." Trick popped a migraine tablet and pulled out his phone. He'd wait for Benjamin Bordain's escort to a cold slab and a second call to Chief Irwin, who'd want to check out the scene himself before the body was hauled away. He watched as Jim headed for the house, both of them filled with the frustration of finding the guy only to lose him and hit another, very dead end.

Jim dreaded the job of having to give the news to his mother. She'd had enough bad news in her life and somehow the words 'I'm sorry for your loss' just didn't cut it. Notifying family was the one job every cop hated. When he entered the house and gave Mrs. Bordain the news she was unusually calm except for the shaking hands that held her cup of tea.

The two of them sat in silence as the sound of sirens grew closer.

"Do you want to say goodbye to your son?"

She shook her head, defeated. "No. I've lost him and he was the only reminder of my late husband. I could look into his eyes and see the remnants of his father's genes in his face. It comforted me."

"I'm so sorry," said Jim, glancing at the photo. Benji had inherited his father's bright blue eyes, but his father's had a warm twinkle in them while Benji's looked as cold as an arctic ice floe despite his smile.

"I want to think he's in the welcoming arms of his father and the good Lord now."

She burst into tears.

Big Jim Bullock had questions for her but now wasn't the time. Mrs. Bordain didn't have the heart to go to the garage to say goodbye to her only son and she was falling apart before his eyes.

She wanted to remember him as the sweet little boy looking up at his mother in the old photograph.

It was easier that way.

"Is there someone you could call to come and be with you?" he asked.

After much thought, she replied: "Reverend Jeske at Cactus Flower Baptist." She reached across to the side table, shaking hands fumbling through her small address book as she pointed to the number. "You call. I can't talk right now."

Jim made the call and the Reverend assured him he was on his way to console his parishioner. He handed Mrs. Bordain his card. "I'll need to ask you a few questions. Call me when you're up to talking. Again, I'm sorry for your loss."

The two of them sat in silence until Reverend Jeske knocked on the door, then Jim went outside, leaving the work of comforting words to the rotund Reverend. Trick stood in the shadows beside the garage as the vehicles approached, sirens blaring. Wrinkles of migraine pain furrowed his brow as he popped another pill and leaned against the building, staring at the weeds beneath his feet as if they held some answer. Was that a shadow he had seen behind a palm tree three doors down?

"You okay?" asked Jim.

"Fucking migraine," he moaned. "Mind if I take the car? I've got to get out of here and find a dark, quiet room. I can't deal with this right now."

"Go. I'll get a ride back with the Chief."

Big Jim saw him look down the street as he headed for the car, popping another pill along the way." He didn't know about migraines. He'd never had one, but looking at Trick he knew they were nasty business.

Chief Irwin's car pulled up, the ambulance not far behind. He and Jim entered the garage and Chief Irwin digested the scene.

"Looks like he fell off the ladder," said Jim.

"Looks that way," said the Chief turning his head towards the ladder, then back to the body on the floor. "Another broken neck. We've sure been collecting a lot of broken necks around here lately. What are the odds? Makes a guy wonder."

Wonder what?

"I see where you're going with this, but sometimes things are just a coincidence, don't you think?"

"C'mon, Jim," he said. "You know as much as I do that there's no such thing as a coincidence. Do you think the kid covered himself with those clothes after he landed?"

"Half covered. As much of a mess as this place is he could have just landed into that pile of stink."

Chief Irwin motioned for the emt's to remove the body after he took some photos of the scene. Too early to call it a crime scene but he was definitely thinking in that direction. He was hard put to figure who would have wanted him dead. A drug deal gone bad? Didn't make much sense. The kid only dealt enough to feed his own habit, so that was unlikely. They needed to find out more about Benji Bordain. Find something. He shrugged. Maybe it was an accident. Maybe it was only a coincidence. But in his experience coincidences rarely happen. They tended to be part of a puzzle, just one more piece to help put the picture together and solve what needed to be solved then put in a cardboard box, closed and forgotten.

As the two men headed towards the car Jim spotted someone down the street. It was only a glimpse, but he definitely saw someone hovering behind a palm tree. As the man peeked out from behind it, Jim zeroed in on him and the first thing he noticed, even at a distance, was the man's large nose.

He took off running in the man's direction as Big Nose high-tailed it in the opposite direction. It didn't take long to catch up with him. "If you run you'll only go to jail tired," he said as he threw him to the ground and cuff him. Jim pushed him down the sidewalk and stuffed him in the back seat of Chief Irwin's car.

"You can't do this," the man protested. "I ain't done nothin' and this is harrassment."

"I can do what I want," said Jim. "I'm at the steering wheel and you're in the back seat, so shut your mouth."

Chief Irwin slid into the driver's seat and they headed back to headquarters as the man with the big nose protested non-stop all the way. His mouth was even bigger than his beak.

Jim had some questions. The guy was definitely one of the images in the Wong video and he had no doubt he held some answers.

TWENTY-ONE

The old Chevy coated itself with desert dust as Cal and Kandi sped down the old road towards Camino Del Diablo. It was the one place where they could go, deserted and unnoticed and free to steal their clandestine times together. It was rare to pass another car along this arid stretch of nowhere so it was the perfect playpen for the young lovers. Kandi ran her bare foot up and down his leg as he drove, letting out a sigh of anticipation. Her times spent with her husband, the Honorable Judge Gareth Lambert, were only tolerable knowing she'd have her time with Cal whenever they had the opportunity. He was her breath of fresh air that broke up the stifling, stale air that filled her bedroom in the mansion back in Agua Verde.

Life couldn't get better. She had the best of both worlds. Putting up with old money-bags was easier knowing Cal would always be waiting for her in the wings.

Cal pulled off to the side of the road at their favorite spot and killed the engine. They looked out at the Tule Mountains in the distance, then she leaned into him, her hand wandering between his legs, her warm breath exhaling as she ran her tongue along his perspiring, salty neck and nuzzled against him. He leaned over, facing her as his hand reached under her t-shirt and caressed her braless skin. She felt like velvet. Warm, wet velvet. They pulled away from each other, got out of the car, opened the rear doors and slid into the back seat like a couple of teenagers at a drive-in movie straight out of the 1960's. Back seats were as good now as they were back then. The perfect place to do the things that parents or spouses never suspected they would ever do.

The forbidden fruit had always been the sweetest fruit of all. And Kandi was ready for a great big, juicy bite. Those old hellfire and damnation preachers would say Eve committed some kind of terrible sin but Kandi would bet Judge Gareth's fat bank account that Eve didn't regret it one damn bit. God wouldn't have made us the way he did unless he'd meant us to use it. Parts and all. And use them she did. Hallelujah, Jesus. Or whoever or whatever the creator might be. Good sex was definitely her manna from heaven. Amen.

Sweaty body slid against sweaty body until the two of them were exhausted and relaxed in each others arms. They rolled down the windows and let the warm desert breeze drift across their bodies, their eyes closed as they listened to the occasional chatter of quails or a gust of wind or the scurry of a lizard across the desert floor break the silence.

"Let's take a walk," Cal said as he struggled to put on his clothes.

Kandi slipped on her shorts and t-shirt and followed him out of the car.

The grit scrunched beneath their sandaled feet as they walked away from the car and into the desert wilderness. It was a beautiful, perfect day. Not too hot for this time of year. Just perfect for the two lovers as they walked hand in hand looking at the occasional wildflower and the clear and cloudless blue sky. A Harris's Hawk perched high on the tip of a gnarled saguaro, keeping an eye out patiently for a tasty lunch to pass his way.

Kandi tripped on something underfoot and as she stumbled Cal caught her. They both looked down.

"Shit. Oh shit," he said when he saw the bony arm protruding from the cracked earth.

"You found me," the voice whispered, but they couldn't hear her.

"This is bad," said Kandi.

"I've waited so long. Will you take me home now? I just want to go home."

The voice of a ghost was hard to hear if you weren't open to hearing it.

"We need to report this," Cal said.

"Report what? That we found some damn skeleton out here?"

"What if it was murder?"

"What if it's been here forever and it's nothing but another nameless crosser? Who'd give a shit?"

"It should be reported Kandi. It's the right thing to do." Cal looked down at the skeletal fingers, the worn hints of red nail polish on the fingertips, the few spots where bits of flesh still clung tenuously to the bone like loose roof shingles. It might be old, but it wasn't that old. And it was a woman, no doubt about that.

"Knock it off Cal! What would you say? Well, I was just out here banging my boss's wife when we stumbled across it? Really? Would you tell them you were screwing the judges wife? Would you actually be willing to put what we have in jeopardy over this nobody?"

She had a point, he had to admit that, but it just didn't sit right with him. The dead woman must have somebody, somewhere who missed her. Didn't they deserve to know? He followed Kandi as she stormed back towards the car. How long did he expect her to wait? About them. He caught up to her, grabbed her arm and spun her around to face him.

"I love you, Kandi, you know that. But how long am I supposed to wait for you to end it with the Judge?"

She'd never before seen anger in his eyes. Those beautiful eyes. "Be patient, okay? You know I love you, but it's not the right time. Not yet."

"When will it be the right time? Is there even such a thing as the right time?"

"When I'm good and ready and not before. I love you Cal, but you need to be patient. Stop pushing me."

"Stop. Don't walk away. Please don't leave me here."

The ghostly whisper went unheard as Cal and Kandi walked away.

"I just want to go home."

Saying okay wasn't easy for him but they'd finally agreed that this day never happened. They got into the car, turned it around and headed back to Agua Verde. A million doubts and questions swam around in his head as he drove in silence. He was beginning to wonder if she really loved him as much as he loved her. Enough to walk away from that rich old man as she kept promising?

He pushed the thoughts away.

"And I don't bang you, Kandi. And I don't screw you. I make love to you. There's a difference."

He waited for her response but was met only with a shrug of her shoulders. But he knew she loved him. The electricity between them was so intense, so wonderful, it couldn't be anything but love. They had something special that most people don't find in a lifetime. It was pure magic for them both.

He swallowed his doubts and shoved them into the back of his mind where he couldn't hear them.

She'd never play him for a fool.

Not Kandi.

TWENTY-TWO

Big Jim Bullock decided to let the guy with the big nose sweat it out in a cell until Tuesday morning. There was no doubt in his mind that this was one of the guys on the video from Jai Wong's store. He had him. Benji wasn't talking but if he shook this guy up enough he might talk. They'd booked him under the name he'd given: Tony Pitassi. Anthony "Tony" Pitassi was another local whose rap sheet was nothing but a list of petty crimes and misdemeanors. Nothing serious in his past, at least nothing for which he'd been caught. His street name was Snorkel, likely because of the nose that took up half his face. Why did young fools always think they needed a street name? Did they think it made them sound tougher than they really were? Dead Benjamin Bordain didn't have a street name, just Benji, like the dog in the old kids movie.

The squad room was half empty as Chief Irwin stood before them. Mackey Hogan was still out on supposed sick leave and Trick Delgado was still at home nursing his migraine in a room with the drapes drawn. Jim and William Washington were separated by several chairs, eyes on the Chief as he spoke.

"We're stuck with a skeleton crew today," he began, "but I expect the two of you to get something substantial accomplished. Things are going too slow and the natives are getting restless. The death of Benjamin Bordain has been ruled a broken neck, likely a drunken accident, but I don't like it. For now though, it is what it is. Officer Washington..."

"Yessir."

"Still nothing to report on the jewelry store robbery?"

"Not yet sir, but I'll keep working on it."

"Work harder." He turned his eyes to Big Jim.

"Good job spotting that Pitassi character yesterday. He's definitely one of those three in the video. I think he's had enough time squirming in that cell so get busy with the interrogation. Find out something. Something that's going to help get Jia Wang's murder tied up in a pretty little bow. Dismissed."

Big Jim Bullock and William Washington rose and headed out of the room. William had given him a sideways glance he couldn't interpret as they walked in opposite directions. Did it mean what he thought it meant? A subtle signal? He could be wrong, but if he was right it made no difference anyway. No difference at all.

Jim headed to the holding cell where "Snorkel" Pitassi had likely spent a very uncomfortable night. The longer they sit in isolation, the more they think, the more unnerved they become, the more willing they are to talk. The silence wears them down.

* * * *

Snorkel squirmed in his seat as Jim Bullock studied him from across the table. The silence was deafening. He couldn't be sure why he was there. Why he had to spend the night in a holding cell with no explanation. With all the shit he'd pulled and gotten away with it could be anything. Or everything.

Jim finally spoke.

"So, tell me, Mr. Pitassi," he said. "Why don't you tell me where you were last Friday morning?"

"Friday? What's today anyway? I kinda lost track, ya' know?"

"Happy Tuesday. Your day of reckoning."

Snorkel shifted in his seat, raised a hand to shelter his eyes against the bright light. "Friday, Friday, Friday," His eyes looked up at the ceiling as if it held the answer. "Oh, I remember Friday. I slept til noon like I always do."

"You sure about that?"

"Yeah, I'm sure. I party at night and sleep away my mornings."

"No little side trips first? Like maybe for a beer run?"

Now it was getting uncomfortable. What did this guy know and how did he know it?

"No, man. Like I said, I'm not a morning guy."

"Ever been in Wong's store?

"What the hell is that?" Little beads of sweat sprouted on his forehead like a teenager breaking out with a case of acne. He wiped his brow with a twitching forearm. An arm with a few festering needle marks and scribbled with crappy jailhouse tattoos that looked more like half-hazzard graffiti than art.

Big Jim Bullock rose and walked over to the player, shoved the video into the slot and hit play. Snorkel raised his eyes and watched as the scratchy image came into focus.

Oh, shit.

"Sure looks like you taking those six-packs from the refrigerator case, don't you think?"

"Not me, man," he said, but he knew he was busted.

"Don't insult my intelligence."

"Okay, so you got me. You gonna charge me with theft?"

Jim pointed towards the close up that flashed in front of the camera.

"And isn't that your friend Benji?"

"That's why the cop cars were in front of his house? Is he here too?"

"He's dead."

Snorkel let out an audible groan.

"So tell me," Jim said. "We know you were there and we know Benjamin Bordain was there, so why don't you tell me who the third guy was? The one white as a bleached sheet."

"I don't get where you're going. I don't know the guy."

"Stop with the crap. You're not being charged with theft, you're going to be charged with murder so you'd better start talking. And you'd better be honest if you want to save your own skin."

"We didn't kill anybody," he insisted. "We didn't!"

"The white guy, who is he?"

"Okay, okay. I don't know his real name. We just call him Whitey the Werewolf."

"And where can we find him?"

"Whitey? He ain't got no home. He just drifted into town and we crossed paths with him when he was looking for a little dope, that's all. Okay, so Benji comes up with the idea the three of us can pick up some extra cash stealing a few things from Wong's. Always just one old chink behind the counter who'd probably not even notice."

"But she did notice, didn't she?" It was a statement more than a question.

"That ain't how it went down. We headed in as the last customer was leaving and when we get inside there ain't nobody behind the counter. So I head for the brew along with Whitey and Benji heads for the smokes. That's when he seen it."

"Saw what?"

"Well, he spots the camera and when he goes up to block it that's when he sees it. He yells at us and we all freak."

"What exactly did he see?"

"The body. He saw the body lying on the floor behind the counter."

"Mrs. Wong?"

"I don't know who she was, but I swear man, she was dead before we got there. We got the hell out of there as fast as we could."

There was something about Tony Pitassi's demeanor that Jim's instincts told him he was telling the truth.

"We might be thieves but we sure as hell ain't murderers," he said.

"Can you describe the customer that was leaving as you were entering?"

"I wish I could but we didn't give him a second glance. All I can say for sure was it was a man."

Another dead end.

"Back to the guy you call Whitey the Werewolf. This time I expect you to tell me where we can find him."

"I told you I don't know. He hightailed it out of town right after that and I never saw him again. For all I know he could be in Fucktardia by now."

"So Whitey just floated away like a house of cards caught in a soft breeze."

"He wasn't a friend. Guys like that, they just wander. They come and go like ghosts and never settle anywhere in particular. They just drift, ya' know?"

Jim Bullock had one suspect in the wind, another one dead and speechless and a third sitting across from him that seemed to be telling the truth. Odds are, they had a suspect, but not one of these three. He wondered who the customer was exiting Wong's. He could have well been the man who killed Jia Wong, but they had no description and a missing tape that might have helped identify him. The only progress on the whole incident was eliminating their prime suspects and that wasn't much.

"I appreciate your cooperation, Mr. Pitassi, you can get up now."

"So I can go?" he exhaled a sigh of relief.

"Sure, you can go right back to the holding cell. You're being charged with theft."

"Not fair," he whined like a kid in a school yard who just lost a game of tag you're it.

"Count your blessings that you're not being charged with more. You've been helpful so I'll do what I can to see that the Judge goes light on you."

Tony Pitassi sighed again, resigned to his fate. He sighed a lot.

"And you have to promise one more thing. Get it together. Keep your nose clean."

"I can. I know I can. This whole thing has scared the holy crap out of me."

Jim could tell that Snorkel meant it. At least at that moment. He really did. Whether he'd be capable of keeping that promise was yet to be seen. Guys like him had burrowed themselves so deeply in that rut that it had become a part of them. Digging themselves out of the hole wasn't easy. He hoped Pitassi had a big enough shovel.

He escorted Tony Pitassi back to the holding cell, grabbed a paperback book from a shelf and handed it to him. Tony looked at him, puzzled.

"It'll help pass the time," he said. "Let reading be your first new habit. You might actually learn something."

"Dude," he replied, like dude was a word for thanks.

That was good enough for Jim.

Maybe there was hope for him after all, he thought as he looked back at the guy burying his big nose into the first page of My Dark Places by James Ellroy.

On second thought, maybe he should have handed the kid a bible. Nah, he'd probably get bored even before Eve ate the forbidden fruit. Ellroy might get his attention enough that he would turn the next page.

TWENTY-THREE

Jim spent the rest of the morning cruising the streets of Agua Verde. Cars with out of state license plates passed him, within the speed limit, as they headed towards the Grand Canyon or Las Vegas or California. Locals who weren't working for the day rode their bicycles or strolled the sidewalks looking in store windows or heading into restaurants for lunch. Some were probably drinking their lunches at Flaming June's or Jalisco's Cantina. The half empty trolley clanged its way up and down the main street. On the surface all was peaceful. And boring. He couldn't do as much as write a traffic citation.

There had been enough action the last few weeks to keep his brain swimming. Jia Wong had been murdered in her store, lying on the floor with a broken neck. The mother of the abused little boy had been found dead in her squalid apartment with a broken neck. Their only suspect, her boyfriend Joey Palermo, had hung himself in the holding cell. The jewelry store had been robbed and William Washington had yet to find a suspect. He and Trick had zeroed in on their suspect, Benji Bordain, in the Wong murder only to have found him dead with a broken neck from a drunken accident. Benji's buddy Snorkel was in the holding cell but it was looking more and more like the trio of hoodlums had nothing to do with her murder.

But who had?

Not a drop of blood, just lots of broken necks and no answers.

But there had been highlights too. He'd rescued Paco, the little homeless puppy of a man, and taken him home to heal. He may have entered his life as a nuisance, but Paco had become a gift he'd never anticipated. Paco had added a ray of sunshine and enjoyed the gallery and all its art as much as he did. Maybe more. Despite the tragedies of Paco's life he managed to maintain a joy and enthusiasm that Jim found not only brave, but downright endearing.

He pulled his car into Trick's driveway and walked up the pathway. When he knocked, he was surprised when Ingrid opened the door, welcoming him in with half a smile and tired eyes rather than her usual welcoming smile. He admired her elegance and composure as he followed her into the kitchen.

She poured him a cup of coffee without having to ask, then sat across from him. Her control was slightly frayed around the edges.

"I stopped in to see how he's doing."

"Lying down. Jim, those headaches are getting worse. This one is so bad that I called in to work so I could stay home with him. The doctor's no help. He just throws more pills at him."

She went silent when Trick entered the room, eyes red and puffy from lack of rest. He looked beat down like he'd just lost a bout in the boxing ring with the great Ali.

"I thought I heard voices," he said with a weak smile as he crossed the room and joined them at the table. Ingrid rose and brought him a cup of coffee.

"Thanks," he said taking the mug from her hand. "I'm feeling better. Much better."

But he didn't look it.

"If you'd like a partner for the rest of the day I'm up to it."

Jim filled him in on the events since they'd found dead Benji Bordain.

"It's as dead as Benji out there, so stay home and rest and I'll see you in the squad room tomorrow morning."

The three of them sat drinking coffee and exchanging small talk, then Jim said his goodbyes, finished out an uneventful day and headed home.

* * * *

Jim opened his unlocked front door and when he went inside he could see Paco standing in the kitchen talking on the phone. He looked up, his expression like the kid caught with his hand in the cookie jar, uttered a few words in Spanish into the phone and quickly hung up.

"Mr. Chim!" Paco ran over and greeted him with a hug. "You are home."

The hug was returned.

"I told you to keep the doors locked. It's dangerous."

"I forget so many things. I am sorry."

"Please. Just try to remember." He felt it was none of his business, but felt the need to ask. "Who was on the phone?"

"The phone. I did not ask permission. I am sorry."

"This is your house too. You don't need my permission. I was surprised you had friends in town, that's all. You never mentioned them."

"*Mi amigos?*" he covered his mouth with his hands and giggled. "No, *mi abuelita!* Oops, in the English. It is so wonderful, Chim. My grandmother, she does not listen to the family. We have been talking but it is our secret. She still loves her Paco even if the family has forbidden me."

It pleased Jim to know that Paco's entire family hadn't abandon him. That there was one person who loved him just as he was. "Call your grandma as often as you want. I'm happy for you. And she's welcome to come visit you here any time. Someday I'd like to meet her. She sounds like a good and special person."

Paco danced around the kitchen, twirling and tapping his feet like a flamenco dancer.

He did a pirouette, opened the refrigerator, then closed its door just as quickly.

"Let's eat dinner and look at art books!"

Ah, the art books. They'd opened a whole new world for him.

"Mexican or Italian?"

"Oh, Chim, you know I'm Mexican. Sometimes you say things silly."

"I was referring to dinner."

"Oh. Whatever's the fastest. And no table. Could we sit in the recliners and listen to that Cougat record while we eat? And then look at the art books?"

Jim nodded.

"I love you, love you, love you, Mr. Chim!"

"I love you, too."

And they both meant it.

TWENTY-FOUR

Trick Delgado's latest headache had finally taken flight, likely in search of another soul to torture. It felt like a living entity come to earth for the sole purpose of burrowing deep into his brain. He wondered how many others were on its hit list. He kissed Ingrid good bye, stopped into the market and picked up a few supplies for his mother, and drove to her home. He felt more optimistic than he had in a long time and he wasn't going to let her get to him. Not today. She'd been calling him *bad* as far back as he could remember. Even when he was a little boy. And he knew he'd never been bad, never. Not even when she whacked him for no reason at all. By the time she grabbed the cans of cat food he had already walked out the door and headed for work.

The cops sat in their chairs listening to the usual orders of the day from Chief Irwin. The Chief was edgy and impatient. There were crimes to be solved and in his eyes they weren't getting the job done. He stopped short of a verbal thrashing, knowing they were doing their best, but it was frustrating just the same.

Big Jim Bullock and Trick Delgado would be teaming up as usual and William Washington had the jewelry store robbery on his menu. As they rose to leave Chief Irwin motioned to Trick. "In my office, Delgado."

Trick shot a puzzled look at Jim, rose with a shrug and followed the Chief into his office. It felt like being called to the Principal's office for passing notes in class. The Chief took a seat behind his desk as Trick stood across from him, wondering what this could be about. Maybe he'd get chewed out for all the headache induced sick days. He couldn't say that he blamed him. Every time they hit he'd disappear for awhile, leaving an already small department even smaller and less able to function. But he couldn't help it.

"Sit," the Chief said.

Trick sat in the chair across from him. "I apologize for yesterday."

"This isn't about yesterday. It's about a whole lot more." The Chief shuffled through the papers on his desk, occasionally looking up as he lined up the papers in a row.

Trick was puzzled to say the least. What the hell had he done?

"This is what I've got, Delgado, and I'm not liking it." He turned the first paper towards Trick, then another and another, hammering each one with his finger as he spoke.

"Jia Wong. You knew her. That's where you stop for your coffee in the morning. Dead. Tina Weston and Joey Palermo. Dead. Your wife Ingrid is handling the case involving their abused son. Benjamin Bordain. Dead. You've arrested the guy numerous times."

"What in the world are you getting at?"

"You have a connection to each on of them Delgado and it doesn't look good."

Trick couldn't believe what he was hearing. "Are you accusing me of…?

"Not yet, but there's no such thing as coincidence and my radar is on high alert. If we weren't so short staffed I'd put you on paid leave until this entire mess is resolved."

"That's crazy. Sir. This is a small town, paths cross. I'll bet every cop you have has dealt with every one of them at one time or another. It's inevitable. Even Wong's. I'll bet they've all arrested Benjamin Bordain at least once. Besides, his death was an accident. Palermo hanged himself in his cell because he'd killed that Tina Weston chick. Hogan was the one who took him back. I don't like Mackey but he was no more responsible for the guy hanging himself than I was."

"So prove me wrong," the Chief gave Trick a look he couldn't decipher but he didn't like it.

"Now get to work," he said, with a wave of dismissal. "And I'll be watching you."

Trick shook his head in total confusion as he rose and left the room. Jim Bullock stood in the other room waiting for him.

"What was that all about?" he asked as they headed out. He could see that Trick was visibly shaken by whatever had taken place behind that closed door.

"It's bullshit, Jim. Total bullshit. He damn near accused me of being guilty. Of all of it. So my paths have crossed with all the victims, but so has everybody else's. Agua Verde's small enough that everybody bumps into everybody sooner or later. It doesn't mean squat."

"It sounds like he's grasping at straws. Could he really be so desperate to get these things solved that he's actually looking at one of his own? Makes no sense to me either."

"He kept giving me the stink-eye. Can you believe it?"

As they slid into the car Trick looked over at Jim.

"Do you think somebody's trying to frame me? Somebody who might think I arrested him one time too many? Somebody who wants to get even?"

"It's a possibility," said Jim. "Tell you what, in our down time we'll go through all our records and see if we can zero in on somebody. Anybody who'd hold a grudge big enough, and has a brain smart enough, to set you up. I'd never thought of that angle before. No reason to."

"Thanks."

"That's what friends are for."

Wednesday was proving to be another less than eventful day. The best they could accomplish was writing a few tickets between tossing ideas back and forth regarding the accusations Chief Irwin had shot at Trick, as lethal as hollow point bullets. None of it made any sense to either of them. All Jim knew was that Trick was incapable of being anything other than a good cop and a good friend.

And Trick knew he didn't do any of it.

Later that afternoon, as the sun threatened to hide behind the mountains for another day, the two men returned to the squad room. They pulled files and stacked them on their desks. They scrutinized them, one file at a time, searching. Hoping they'd find an answer. Find someone with a grudge big enough to make Trick Delgado look like a dirty cop. A killer cop.

There were still plenty of files to go through when they called it a day.

Trick had Ingrid to go home to.

And Jim, although even his best friend didn't know, had Paco.

In the distance, dark clouds were drifting in from Mexico, holding the promise of much needed rain. But the clouds, combined with the summer heat, were tricksters. Sometimes the raindrops arrived, giving the desert floor a welcome drink. Sometimes it was only virga, a strange phenomena where rain would evaporate from the heat before ever reaching the ground. Jim loved the smell of creosote when the wet beads fed the soil and the dead stalks of the ocotillo burst to life with hundreds of tiny green leaves and branches tipped with bright orange flowers that looked like flames.

It was nearing dark when Jim pulled into his driveway. Paco, his little sparrow, raced out to the car to greet him with his endearing enthusiasm. He held Jim's hand tighter than usual as they entered the house, then pulled the big man to where the newspaper lay open on the kitchen table.

"Look, Chim, look!" he said. Jim looked down to the small article and read it. Not the usual announcement for the gallery, but a small boxed ad stating that there would be another special showing of Doobie's art on Friday night. The last show had been a near sellout and the artist must have been busy, as the gallery owner had insisted, coming up with new paintings to fill the empty walls.

"Can we? Can we, please?"

Jim thought of how much his savings had dwindled at the last show. He'd given in and bought several paintings for Paco. But he had made Paco so happy.

"Is okay Mr. Chim? We go see more Doobie? Please." He gave Jim that cute, irresistible pout that melted the big man's heart every time.

"Okay," Jim said finally, knowing he'd better bring his checkbook.

TWENTY-FIVE

Big Jim Bullock and Trick Delgado spent Thursday cruising the streets of Agua Verde, keeping their eyes open for the elusive Whitey the Werewolf who was likely in a different state by then. But they looked nonetheless. You never know what the truth really is. Cops are lied to all the time. Enough that they can spot a lie as easily as a cockroach in a bin of white flour. Suspects had "tells" just like gamblers, their body language giving them away. A glance downward as their brain formed a lie, a moment of rising anger that told a cop he'd hit a nerve and was on the right track. But there was the rare time a cop got snookered. Jim thought Tony "Snorkel" Pitassi had told him the truth, instinct said so, but even instinct lied once in awhile. He had to be sure, so he kept his eyes open in case the ghost was still lurking in the shadows.

Jim's heart sank as they drove past Wong's. The white fabric was still draped above the door, the gong still nailed next to it. The signs of mourning remained but the sign in the window said OPEN. Even in his heartbreak Mr. Wong had no choice but to reopen for business. He had bills to pay and a little boy named Winston to feed and raise alone. Jim and Trick owed him an answer as to who would kill his beloved wife. For no reason. It was looking less and less like it had been for beer and cigarettes which pushed the two cops farther away from the answer.

"Do you want to stop in to see Mr. Wong?" Jim asked Trick. He was relieved when Trick declined. He had no news for him. None at all, but when he did go inside he wanted it to be because he'd solved the crime. It would do nothing to make Mr. Wong feel better, but it at least would give him the strength he needed. There was no such thing as closure. Just justice or revenge. The pain remains raw, just beneath the surface, and every time it rises the pain is as strong as it was the day it all happened. That never went away. But Mr. Wong needed to move forward, for his son as well as for himself. When someone is murdered it isn't one death. It scars and damages and in some way destroys the lives of everyone the victim's life had touched. Friends and family are never the same again. A piece of them is lost forever.

Jim steered the car down other streets. He passed Flaming June's and thought about the night he'd rescued Paco from his viscous beating. Another failure as the gang that enjoyed gay bashing and beating up on the homeless still lurked in the shadows beyond their grasp. They'd nail the little bastards sooner or later. The sooner the better. But they sure weren't going to find them in the light of day. People like that thrived in the safety of darkness unseen, like vampires waiting for their next meal of blood, energized by the metallic taste of it.

Jim turned on the wipers as the first drops of rain hit the dusty windshield, dancing slowly downward as it smeared the desert grit across the glass.

Their day ended at their desks, sifting through files looking for who might have set up Trick. The files of "possibles" they'd set aside was as small as a short stack of pancakes.

TWENTY-SIX

On Friday night Doobie held a glass of wine as he leaned against the bar. Jim and Paco greeted him as they entered the gallery. Doobie welcomed the two men, the only ones he'd met in Agua Verde that he was beginning to consider friends. He smiled, thinking how unlikely that he, an aging hippie who hated cops would ever befriend one. Jim Bullock's little sidekick Paco was easy. He'd had plenty of gay friends back in San Francisco. No problem there, but a cop? Well, he'd finally had to admit that this cop was different. He refilled his glass and continued with the distasteful task of working the room and schmoozing with the other customers. He hated openings as much as he hated the hot Agua Verde summers. Both sucked and made him yearn for the thick, chill fogs of the life he'd left behind. He had to remind himself that the place had morphed into something no longer recognizable. That's why he'd left. The gallery owner never failed to remind him, the money in the out of towners pockets put the food on his table. Both their tables. Play nice. He hated that as much as he hated Agua Verde summers. Both sucked.

Jim pulled Paco away from the wall where he was standing admiring the new artwork and walked him over to Doobie. At the last gallery opening he'd said something that hurt Paco and there was something important he needed to say.

"Doobie, I'd like to reintroduce you to Paco. He's not my cousin and he's not a rodeo clown."

Doobie cracked a smile as Jim continued.

"Paco is my partner. My lover. My friend."

Paco grinned from ear to ear, a big Cheshire cat grin. He was surprised at Jim's admission. It meant he was no longer ashamed of him.

"Pleased to meet you, Paco," said Doobie as he reached out and shook his hand. Then he turned to Jim. "I already knew that, Jim. You didn't fool me for a minute. When the big, bad macho cop came in with Paco I saw the way you looked at him. You're eyes gave you away. Don't worry, you're secret's safe with me."

"I'm getting tired of secrets," he replied.

Doobie refilled his glass, savoring the taste and the slight buzz as Paco returned to the wall filled with new watercolors, his eyes flitting from painting to painting and back again. Jim stood behind him, enjoying the pleasure Paco got from the bold colors. He felt, in some way, like a teacher who had opened a magical door for him.

"This one, this one!" Paco said pointing to the painting and turning to look at Jim. "Please Mr. Chim?" Jim emptied his wine glass, thinking of his checkbook. Seeing the excitement on Paco's face. He studied the painting Paco had zeroed in on and was glad he was only pointing at one. It was the one that had been in the paper announcing tonight's show. The colors were bright purple against canary yellow. Red against blue. A trolley, a passing car, a bus. It would have been his own choice. It was ultimate Doobie.

They flagged Doobie over, who remembered that last time they'd insisted taking their purchases home. His first sale of the night, the first blank space on the wall. They were so fucking easy, the cop and the kid. But they were the only customers he looked forward to seeing. They weren't the usual art snobs. They were real. Jim and Paco were rebels and he liked that. Jim giving the system the finger at the same time he wore the uniform. Paco flaunting his gayness in a macho universe. His old beatnik San Francisco would've loved them.

Paco pointed to the painting and Doobie reached up and removed it from the wall.

Looking towards the door, Doobie saw the man standing there. Despite his immaculate desert casual clothes, he looked tough and greasy. Even seedy. The clothes did a poor job of hiding the man, who'd have looked more at home in cheap polyester. His demeanor was intimidating as piercing dark eyes darted around the room. Instinctively, Doobie averted his eyes as he carried the painting Paco, well Jim really, was buying and headed for the register.

As agitated as a junkie itching for his next fix, a gruff voice said, "I want this one." It was the sleazy man loudly summoning anyone who would listen. He was pointing to the painting in Doobie's hands, the one with the trolley.

"Sorry, it's already sold," he said.

The man drew attention to himself as he bellowed "I'll pay you double!"

"I said it's sold," Doobie repeated, thinking: One hell of a popular painting-should have done three.

"Triple," the man growled. His eyes were menacing, glaring right through Doobie. Heads turned toward the commotion. Big Jim Bullock took two steps in their direction but the gallery owner got there first, trying to diffuse things as tempers rose. He reaffirmed that the painting was already sold and not available at any price. Seeing all the attention focused on him the man stormed out the door. He hadn't meant to create a scene. Just the opposite. He knew he'd acted stupidly, but self-discipline had never been his strong suit. He just wanted the damn painting. He needed that painting.

Doobie smiled. A painting sold. Some unexpected excitement, which in retrospect was entertaining. Especially now that the creep was gone. Hell, the night was looking up.

* * * *

Big Jim Bullock didn't notice the car shadowing in the distance as he and Paco headed back home. The rain was falling harder now, blurring the windshield and street lights and making the darkness of night even darker. He kept his eyes on the road, tuning out the distraction of the *mariachi* music on the radio and Paco's non-stop chatter.

Before exiting the car, Jim carefully wrapped his jacket around the painting to protect it from the rain, then they both bolted into the house.

Paco refused to retire until they found a spot on the wall for his latest acquisition, paid for by his mentor. He wanted it dead center, so Jim took down a few other paintings, hung it where it would be the focal point on the wall. He drove more nails through the wall as he rearranged the placement of the other ones on either side of the trolley painting.

Paco sat in the recliner watching as Jim worked, constantly commenting on how beautiful the wall had become and how much he loved Jim.

"Tonight you made me twice happy. *Uno, dos*," he said.

"How's that?"

"The painting, *si*. But you told Jim I wasn't your cousin. You told him who I am and I know you are now proud of me. I'm no longer what you hide."

"I've had enough hiding. It's making me tired. Very tired."

"Chim is tired? You want we should go to the bed now?"

That was welcome music to Jim's ears. He was burning for bed.

And Paco's fragile body lying next to his own.

TWENTY-SEVEN

Cal loved Kandi. Despite it being wrong, it felt so right. Under normal circumstances he never would have gotten involved with a married woman, especially when her husband was not only his boss but the town's judge as well, but she drew him in and he couldn't resist her. He wasn't fond of the judge, who never hid the fact that he viewed Cal as beneath him on the social ladder. It bothered Cal, even though the pay was good. Cal was an honest man and felt people should be judged by their character rather than their financial status. Kandi wasn't like that.

Not reporting the body they found in the desert was wrong and no matter how hard Cal tried, he couldn't come up with a reason to rationalize his silence as being the right thing to do.

Maybe the body was a crosser from long ago, but maybe it wasn't. That wasn't his call to make.

Kandi had sworn him to silence for fear her affair with him would be discovered. He was getting frustrated with her straddling the fence regarding when she was going to leave Judge Lambert to build a life with him, but he was a patient man and willing to wait. She was worth it. There had to be a way to do what needed to be done without involving her. It had been eating at him since their last trip to the desert. He was unable to get the image of the pleading, bony hand from his mind. Somebody, somewhere might be missing her; wondering where she was. A parent? A child? A spouse? He imagined the pain, the not knowing, that someone, somewhere, might be going through.

His silence wasn't right.

When Cal entered the police station he looked around the empty room. It wasn't too late to change his mind. He took a deep breath and squared his shoulders.

"Hello?" he called out. "Is anybody there?"

Chief Irwin rose from his desk and walked into the squad room. The young man was standing there, looking apprehensive and nervous.

"Can I help you?"

"I need to report something."

"I'm Chief Irwin. And you?"

"Calvin Armstrong, sir."

The Chief had Cal follow him into his office and motioned for him to sit in the chair across from his desk. The Chief reached for his pen and notepad. "What seems to be the problem, son?"

Cal told him how he had stumbled across the body in the desert out at Camino del Diablo. He was met with a puzzled look.

"What in the world were you doing out there?"

"Sometimes I just like to get away from town. I like to go out in the desert and hike. Just walk around where I can listen to the quiet and be alone," he lied. That kept Kandi out of the picture. And it eased his conscience even if he had to manufacture a few of the details. A minor omission, he told himself. Not really an outright lie.

"There was a skeletal arm sticking out of the ground. I don't think it was there forever. I could tell it was a woman. There was a bit of red nail polish on the tip of her fingernails." The memory made him shudder.

"Can you drive out with me and show me where?"

"I'd rather not. It kind of spoiled the peace of the place for me, you know? And I have a job I need to go to." Cal looked up at the Arizona map on Chief Irwin's wall. "Could I just show you on the map? I know right where it is."

"I guess that'll do for now, but I might need to talk to you again."

Cal and Irwin both rose and walked over to the wall. He pointed to the spot where he and Kandi always pulled over. "I stop for my hikes right there," he said, pointing to the spot. "You pull over there, then walk north into the desert. She's only a four, maybe five minute walk. You can't miss it."

"Okay, we'll definitely send someone out there."

Cal walked towards the door, relieved to have it off his mind, and anxious to leave.

"Before you go," said Chief Irwin, "I'm going to need your name and address for my report. And a contact number if we need to talk again."

Call gave him the information, which included his cell phone number. He never mentioned Kandi. He never mentioned he worked for Judge Lambert. He'd done what needed to be done and hurt no one in the process.

He felt like a heavy weight had been lifted from his shoulders when he walked out the door and onto the street. A scattering of puddles dotted the ground from the recent rain. The faint aroma of moisture still clung to the air, but the sky was cloudless and the brightest, bluest blue he'd ever seen.

TWENTY-EIGHT

The day had been cloudless and sunny, but three fat raindrops slithered down the windshield like diaphanous snakes as Jim Bullock looked up at his house. Darkness was blanketing the earth, so it was unusual for the lights to be off. The house should have been lit up with loud music playing at this hour. And Paco hadn't opened the door and rushed to his car to greet him. His cop antenna rose. He exited the car cautiously, looking to his left and then his right as he headed up the walk to the front door and turned the knob. For once Paco had remembered his safety precaution to lock up. Jim put his key in the slot, slowly opened the door, and flipped on a light as he entered.

He was met with a sense of emptiness and foreboding that screamed and whispered simultaneously somewhere deep within his very core.

The hairs rose on the back of his neck as he unsnapped his holster and pulled out his gun. He held it tightly, hand on the trigger, as he walked through the rooms turning on lights as he walked. The kitchen was empty but the table was neatly set in preparation for the dinner that he could smell burning on the stove. He removed the pot from the burner, turned off the flame, and sat the pot to the side. *Menudo,* a mix of hominy and tripe. A dish Paco loved that Jim didn't have the heart to tell him he thought was downright ghastly. A vase of brittle bush sat in the center of the table. The pretty yellow flowered weeds that Paco had come to love.

Silence, but for the scratch, scratch, scratch of needle against vinyl coming from the living room. He flipped on another light as he entered, scanning the room with his eyes and gun.

Then he looked down.

Paco lay on the living room floor, a large puddle of blood seeping into the area rug beneath and around his lifeless body. All thoughts of forensics and not disturbing a crime scene left Jim as he fell to the floor and cradled Paco in his arms.

An agonized scream burst from deep within him, tears streaming down Big Jim Bullock's face as he sat on the floor and rocked his broken little sparrow.

Why? What had this sweet innocent done to anyone to deserve this?

"I'm sorry," he said. "I'm a cop. I'm supposed to protect people but why couldn't I protect you?" Shame, rage, guilt and anguish whirled through his brain as frantic and disorienting as a Jackson Pollack painting.

The pain drilled into his bones, a hurt deeper than he could ever have imagined possible.

Reluctantly, he gently laid Paco back onto the floor so that he could do what needed to be done. He rose, walked over to the phone, lifted it from the cradle with a shaking hand and made the call. Then he scoured the rest of the house, room by room, in case the monster who'd done this was still on the premises. The house was empty except for Jim and Paco and the shattered glass on the floor where the killer had broken in through the sliding door.

He re-holstered his gun, walked back to the living room and lay down on the floor next to Paco's cold body. A body that had been so warm and filled with life.

Why?

* * * *

All three were there. Chief Irwin, Trick Delgado and William Washington. When they entered the living room Big Jim was on the floor cradling the body of the small, dead man. Jim was rocking him and as he turned his head, they saw the tears rolling down his cheeks.

Trick walked over to him, reached down and rubbed his shoulder. "You need to get up. Let go so we can do our work."

"What happened?" asked William Washington.

"When I came home I found him. Like that."

Chief Irwin looked at the pile of shattered glass while Trick took photos. Lots of them. The paramedics walked in with their equipment and a stretcher to take Paco away. Forever. Jim was cradling Paco in his arms for one last time when the door flew open, slamming against the wall with a bang as Mackey Hogan entered the house, wearing wrinkled civilian cloths and his service revolver at his belt.

Reality sunk in and Jim rose, walked over to the recliner and sat down, cupping his face with his hands as Paco was laid on the stretcher. Paco was gone. There was no bringing him back. And now they knew, all of them. His private life was no longer private. But it didn't matter any more. None of it. Only that his Paco was gone and left a big cavernous hole deep inside of him. He needed to find out who and why. He wanted revenge.

"Well, well, look-y here," said Mackey Hogan. "Tough Big Jim Bullock's nothing but a silly faggot."

"What the hell are you doing here, Hogan? You're on medical leave," said the Chief.

"I heard it on the scanner and had to see what was going on. And surprise, surprise what do I walk in on but a big fairy on the floor crying like a baby."

William Washington reached Mackey first, shoving him so hard that Mackey lost his balance and did a backwards dance before landing ass first onto the floor. William kicked him, then Trick Delgado walked over and kicked him again for good measure. "Shut the fuck up,"

said Trick. "Don't you have one touch of humanity in you?"

Chief Irwin walked over, unusually calm as he reached out, grabbed Mackey's hands and helped him to his feet.

"Thanks, Chief."

Chief Irwin held out his hand again. "Give it to me. Now."

"What?"

"Your gun," he said. "And your badge."

"What the hell for?"

"You're medical leave has expired. You're fired. As of right now."

"You can't do that," he said, confused and defiant as the Chief, William Washington and Trick Delgado stood together silently staring him down. "You can't."

"It's done. You're done." said the Chief.

"Where am I going to go?"

"Straight to the fires of hell as far as I'm concerned."

"Night watchman would be a perfect fit for your people skills," chimed in William.

"Uh, Chief?"

"What now?"

"A letter of recommendation?"

"You've got to be shitting me."

Reluctantly, Mackey turned over his gun and badge. The men stared holes through him as he turned and walked out the door.

"Not a moment too soon," said Trick.

"He'll be trouble wherever he lands," said William.

Chief Irwin walked over to where Jim sat in the recliner. "We'll handle things from here," he said. "Take a few days off. Take as much time as you need."

"No," he said. "I want to catch the son of a bitch who did this."

"Not in the state you're in," the Chief said. "Take some time to clear your head and then we can talk."

One by one they said their good-bye's to Jim. There was no judgment, just sympathy and support for their fellow officer. The room emptied, leaving Jim alone with nothing but the bloodstains on the floor. Looking at the wall, he stared at the blank space where the latest Doobie painting had hung. Why, if it had been a burglary, would someone take one painting and leave everything else? It made no sense. What was so special about that painting? That one little painting?

Then he remembered the greaseball at the gallery. How the man's anger took hold when he couldn't have that painting. There had to be a connection. And Jim was going to find out what. He looked at the clock. It was after eleven so it would have to wait until tomorrow. He leaned back in the recliner and dozed off. The night was restless, his brain was filled with nightmarish dreams, waking and sleeping and waking again until all went thankfully dark.

He awoke early and disoriented, wondering if it had all been a bad dream. The drying bloodstain on the floor gave him his answer. Seconds stretched like hours as he watched the clock hands move slowly until they finally reached ten a.m. The gallery was finally open. He punched in the number and the gallery owner answered. Jim's questions flew through the phone like a barrage of gunfire.

He was trying to be helpful, but the answers came slowly and there were few.

No, the creep hadn't signed the guest book.

They were just glad to have ushered the lowlife out the door and end the disruption.

It was bad for business.

As if Jim gave a damn about the guy's cash register.

Different people had different priorities, but you'd think a dead customer would be somewhere near the top of the list. But for some greedy bastards money trumped anything else.

At least the gallery owner was cooperative when Jim asked for Doobie's number.

Jim wrote the number down on his note pad and hung up the phone.

He had another number to call.

TWENTY-NINE

Doobie opened the door and invited the cop in. He didn't like company. But Big Jim Bullock had called and there was desperation in the cops voice. He needed to talk. They sat on the couch as Yoriko poured them warm sake and cats marched across their laps. Doobie was saddened over the news of Paco's murder. He'd been an endearing little fellow, but most of all he was sad for Jim.

"There's got to be something about that painting," Jim said. "That was the only thing missing from the house. I keep thinking about it, but in all honesty, I don't remember it that well. There was a trolley and a bus. Pretty colors. Nothing that stood out. Why was it important enough to kill for?"

Doobie couldn't figure it either. They sat in silence for a few minutes. Yoriko kept fondling the sash on her kimono and sipping her sake. Doobie sat down his cup and rose with a jolt. "Let's go to my studio, Jim. I remember I painted that one last week. I wasn't even finished when the heat set in. My paint was drying too fast so I took some photos and went to my car. Sometimes I just take photos and reference them for paintings later. I always keep copies filed in my computer."

They entered the studio and Doobie sat down, booted up the computer and clicked on the file. Several photos of his art popped up but one in particular stood out clear as a bell. A trolley, a passing car, the ass end of a bus. Jim stared at it. Trolley. Bus. An old red Chevy Lumina with the first three letters of the license plate. He could see the jewelry store in the background.

"The car. It's got to be about the car," Jim said. "But I can't read all the plate."

"Wait," Doobie said. "There's some photos I worked from." He switched screens and found them. On one of them the license number was more clear, only a few numbers blurred.

"When did you say you snapped those?"

"It was the week sometime before the last showing. Wait. It would have been a Saturday."

"The day of the jewelry store robbery."

"Oh yeah, I remember the sirens. Loud as hell as I was getting into my car."

The two men looked at more photos. There were a few more of the Lumina. And in one of them the license plate on the passing car was as clear as a soothsayer's vision. Bingo.

Doobie clicked, highlighting the car and trolley shots and hit print.

The two men waited as the printer slowly spat out the papers, then Doobie handed them to Jim.

"You've been a big help," Jim said as he took the photos.

"I just hope you catch the bastard."

"Believe me, I will."

He thanked young Yoriko for her hospitality and headed for his car. He revved up the engine and headed for the mortuary.

There were arrangements that needed to be made.

He returned to the mortuary a second time once Paco's body was released. Paco's favorite painting should be buried with him. The painting he loved. But the painting was as gone as Paco.

The painting that had cost so much more than the check Jim had written to purchase it.

There would be no church farewell. Just a simple grave side service. He'd put a small notice in the local paper, but Jim figured he'd be the only one in attendance besides the liberal local priest he'd found willing to preside over a service for the fallen Catholic. Once a Catholic, always a Catholic.

Paco would have liked that.

THIRTY

Jim laid the yellow flowered brittle bush blossoms that Paco had loved onto the coffin next to the roses and chrysanthemums and wide red satin ribbons. As difficult as it was, he was holding himself together. The priest looked around for the other guests. The ones that would never come. Then Jim turned and saw them approaching. It was Chief Irwin, William Washington and his best friend Trick Delgado with his wife Ingrid. They all held flowers, walked over and placed them atop the coffin, nodding silently at Jim. A rainbow of flowers overflowed adding hope and love and acceptance to the sad occasion. They had all come, for him and for Paco. They stood beside him as the priest recited a short, tasteful sermon then stood with them, frozen in the moment, as the coffin was slowly lowered into the ground.

Jim threw a handful of dirt onto the descending coffin. Another handful of dirt followed, from somewhere behind him.

Then another.

He turned, surprised.

"You are Paco's *abuelita,"* he said to the old Mexican woman. The tears in her eyes flowed like little rivulets down the crevices of her wrinkled, weather-worn face, a face that was a roadmap of a hard and difficult life. A face that had seen so many of the sorrows and tragedies along life's journey and had somehow survived them all. Her face told a tale of strength and determination, but her dark brown eyes reflected a gentleness, a kindness that reminded him of Paco.

"And you are Jim, the man Paco called his angel. Thank you for loving him."

"I am his brother, Manuel," said the young man who stood next to her. He reached out to shake Jim's hand, a hand covered in gang tattoos. "I loved him too."

"Manuel, he wants to talk to you," said the grandmother.

"Just a minute," Jim said. "Wait here. Don't leave."

"Si, uno momento."

He walked over to his fellow officers and Ingrid and thanked them for coming. They all reassured him they were here for him then headed toward their cars as he walked back to where Paco's grandmother and brother were waiting.

"I thought being in a gang made me tough, made me special somehow," Manuel began. "I was wrong. Paco was the one I should have been looking up to. He was always the good one. He never hurt anybody. He was always kind. My gang thought beating up the queers and the homeless was fun. Great fun. But I got my wake up call when one of the victims was my own little brother. They weren't tough. They were heartless bullies. I want no part of it. Of them. But I don't know how to get away, where to start."

"He wants a new life. A good life," said the grandmother. "You saved our Paco. Can you save my Manuel?"

Jim thought for a minute, unsure what to say. Then he yelled out to Trick and Ingrid in the distance just as they were getting into their car.

"Trick! Ingrid!" He motioned them to come back.

When they reached them, Jim introduced Manuel and Paco's grandmother. "Let's all go over to Bad Sandy's for some coffee," he said. "There's some things we need to talk about and I can't think of a better place."

* * * *

The five of them squeezed into the duct taped booth, Paco's grandmother and Manuel on one side, Jim and Trick and Ingrid on the other. Jim insisted they order something to eat, so they read the tattered menus. When Bad Sandy walked over they gave him their orders and Jim added, "And bring coffee. Lots of coffee. I think we're going to be here for awhile."

"What's going on?" asked Trick.

"Manuel here, he's part of the gang that's been eluding us. The bashers."

"So why aren't we booking him?"

Grandma looked around nervously, as did Manuel, like they'd just been caught in a trap.

"Manuel never took part in that," Jim said. "And he wants out."

"Then give us names," Trick said, staring the man down.

"I can't do that." Manuel was looking scared. "If I did that I could never go home. I can't be a snitch. They'd hunt me down and kill me and there's nowhere else for me to go."

"Tone it down, Trick," said Jim. "I think I have the solution. Maybe. Just maybe."

Jim motioned Sandy over to the table where he loomed over them like an ominous shadow. Grandma and Manuel didn't know what to think about the big, bad white man.

"Sandy here was like you once, Manuel," Jim said, then asked Sandy if he could tell Manuel his story.

Sandy shrugged. "Sure, no problem."

"Sandy spent half his life behind bars," Jim began, "and figured he'd spend the rest of it there too. It had become his home, his life, his comfort zone. But the last time he got out he found the strength to turn his life around. Like you're trying to do, Manuel. We helped him get a job. A real job and he worked his ass off and kept his nose clean. Eventually he saved up enough money to buy this little café. Right next to the police station. We supported him then and the whole department supports him now."

"See," said Grandma. "You can do it too. You are strong."

"Could you use an extra set of hands around here?" Jim asked Sandy.

"Sure wouldn't hurt."

"You couldn't have a better mentor," Jim said to Manuel.

"You have a job, Manuel," said the Grandma. "*Gracias,* Jim. You are a good man. And you Mr. Sandy, I can't thank you enough."

A man of few words, Sandy just shrugged his shoulders.

"Now about those names," said Trick.

"I can't do it. I'd be a dead man."

"And I'd lose both my grandsons," said the Grandma.

Big Sandy stood there listening to the conversation, shifting his massive weight from one foot to the other then finally spoke.

"I've got a room in the back," he said. "It's not much, but you can stay there until you get things together." He paused, then added: "And I'll show you the ropes. It ain't all that hard once you put your mind to it."

"It's a miracle!" said Grandma, slapping her hands together then crossing herself as she turned her eyes upward and uttered a prayer of thanks in Spanish.

They worked on their meals between small talk and Sandy refilled their coffee cups. One of the worst days of Jim's life looked like it might have a happy ending. Or at least the beginning of one. Sandy took Manuel to the back and showed him around. Jim and Ingrid and Trick chatted and the Grandma slowly worked her way through her lunch. She was a slow eater who paused to savor every bite, smiling to herself as she ate. There was a joy to her face that made her look twenty years younger. The last thing Jim had wanted was being a rescuer again, but one look at the old woman's face and he was glad he stepped up. He did it for himself, for the Grandma who loved her grandsons, but most of all he did it for Paco.

Sandy and Manuel walked over to the table. Sandy put the check down. As they rose to leave Manuel gave his *abuelita* a heartfelt hug. She reassured him that she'd return with some of his belongings. She wouldn't tell the *familia* where he was. Trust in them was lost when they kicked out Paco. Maybe someday they could reconnect with him, when things were safer, but for now she was his lifeline.

And Grandma knew best.

“I’ll come by the station tomorrow,” Manuel said to Trick, “and give you those names.”

THIRTY-ONE

Monday had been a bust for Chief Irwin. They'd all put things on the back burner for the funeral. Supporting a fellow officer had taken priority over all else, as it should have. This morning he stood before his minimal group of officers. His skeleton crew. He had violent crimes that needed solving. Agua Verde wasn't used to murders and the natives were getting restless, as was he. Petty crimes were the norm, people dealt with that unless they were the ones getting their homes or shops robbed. But recent events had brought local crime to a new level.

He looked around the room. William Washington, Trick Delgado, and Jim Bullock. That was it. He could use at least three more men but that wouldn't happen. He could probably manage someone to replace Mackey Hogan, eventually. Having Mackey gone was better than having him here. What morale they had was definitely lifted in his absence and he hadn't been much help when he'd been there. He'd been more disruptive than useful, but when you've got one applicant there weren't any options, so he'd hired him.

And he'd fired him with no regrets.

Jim spoke up. "Chief, I have a lead on the jewelry store robbery. I'd like to work on that with William today, if that's okay. I know it's his case, but together I think we can make some headway."

"Is that good with you William?"

"Yessir."

"Done."

"Delgado," said the Chief, "think you can work solo?"

"Sure, and I want to keep working through those files."

"You're the only one I have on the street today. At least for now. So you're left with cruising the town. The files can wait." Trick didn't hide his disappointment. He wanted his nose in those files. He wanted to figure out who was trying to set him up for the murders and the sooner the better. But even a department as small as theirs had some pecking order. What the Chief ordered he had to do.

No questions asked.

"Dismissed."

Trick headed out the door to cruise the streets of Agua Verde, but his mind was on the murders. The murders that he was certain Chief Irwin suspected him of committing. It was crazy, but crazier things happen. Not only was he determined to solve them, a big feather in his cap, but he had to prove his own innocence in the Chief's eyes. What could have even made the Chief go there? It had to be desperation. But the Chief's desperation had planted its own desperation in Trick and it made him uneasy.

Uneasy in a way he hadn't felt in a long time. It was a feeling he didn't like. The first little throbs of an impending headache danced in his brain. This time he'd nip it in the bud. Outsmart the bastard. He slid into the seat of his squad car, opened the glove compartment and pulled out his bottle of pills. He dry swallowed two, then a third for good measure.

Trick watched as Chief Irwin walked out the door, headed for Bad Sandy's.

Inside the squad room Jim and William hovered over the computer. Jim read off the license plate of the red Chevy Lumina from the small piece of paper as William keyed in the letters and numbers.

And they both waited.

Bingo.

The computer brought up the registered owner. They were surprised he was a local. If Viktor Vlasik was still the owner. And an address, if that was still Viktor Vlasik's address. People like that had a tendency to forget, or ignore, the little rules honest people followed without question. Jim wrote down the address and the two of them headed out.

They'd lucked out.

The faded red Lumina was parked in the driveway collecting desert dust that had turned to muddy streaks from the recent rains.

When they banged on the door there was no answer, so they banged again. Harder this time. They heard someone inside.

"We can't enter without a warrant," William mumbled.

"I thought I heard someone in distress. You heard it too, didn't you?"

They gave each other a knowing smile, squared their shoulders before slamming into the door. Slivers of wood flew through the air from the shattered door frame as they gave it a final kick.

The two men entered the room, guns drawn.

Jim immediately recognized the bastard from the gallery. The man who had killed Paco. Viktor Vlasik stood frozen, cowered against a wall, eyes flitting around the room, desperate for an exit route. Jim flew through the air and tackled him when he tried to bolt. The man landed with a thud, the big cop on top of him.

Jim's eyes scanned the room as he reached for his handcuffs.

There was still jewelry from the heist scattered on the table next to some crack cocaine and a gun. A knife lay next to it. The painting was on the floor, leaning against a table leg.

Paco's painting. Just the thought infuriated him.

Viktor was bloodshot, weak and wasted. Jim clicked the cuffs on. The man's body language said he'd given up. It was over. But it wasn't over for Jim who still held him in a hammerlock, yelling in his ear.

"You dumb fucking junkie! You traded a couple years in the slammer for life—over this?" He looked over at the painting that had given Paco such joy. The painting that had cost him his life. William stood and watched as Jim's eyes filled with tears, his brain blazing with rage. He tightened his forearm against Viktor's neck, increased the pressure against his throat, made the weasel slobber like a St. Bernard as he gasped for mercy.

It was all so unnecessary.

No one would ever have made the connection.

It felt good, too good, as Jim pushed tighter and tighter until the man's eyes bulged.

"Back off, Jim!" yelled William.

"I'm going to kill the bastard."

It came into focus and William realized this wasn't just the jewelry store robber, but the same man who had murdered Jim's friend.

"Back off," he repeated. "This scumbag isn't worth it."

But he was worth it. Jim could have killed him in a heartbeat, laughing at the sound of vertebrae cracking as the man's life force drained from his worthless, ignorant body. A body that reeked of last week's sweat and this morning's fix.

"Stop!"

Jim hesitated, then heeded the other cop's words and let go as the man gasped for a breath that might have easily been his last. William pulled Viktor up from the floor with a rough jerk.

Not killing him on the spot was the hardest thing Jim had ever done. The son of a bitch was still breathing while his beautiful Paco lay stiff and cold in his grave. What was fair about that? He looked around the dining room again and sighed, staring at the painting with its blurred license plate. His rage continued to sizzle just beneath the surface as William handed him the prisoner, knowing Jim should at least have the pleasure of leading the guy to the squad car. And he did, shoving him along the way, opening the back door, and making sure Viktor bumped his head hard as he threw him into the back seat like yesterday's dirty laundry.

The door shut with such force that William was surprised it didn't break the windows.

He approached Jim where he stood and put an arm around his shoulders. "You did the right thing," he said. "But I don't blame you."

"Blame me? I wanted to kill him. I should have killed him."

"I can imagine what you've been going through."

"You can't begin to imagine."

"I think it's time I told you a story. No, I'll never know exactly what you're feeling, no one will, but I have a pretty good idea. When I was in Detroit my friend was killed. Just one more senseless death from being in the wrong place at the wrong time and taking a stray bullet. Damon wasn't just my friend, he was my lover. I wanted to kill. Somebody, anybody. I knew then that it was time to move on. To leave Detroit behind me. That's what landed me in Agua Verde, Jim. I needed to save myself."

Jim turned and looked into William's dark, sad eyes. "I had no idea."

"We're more alike than you realize. We both believe our private lives are best kept to ourselves."

"But it doesn't matter anymore."

"No, it doesn't. I can see that now."

They got into the squad car as their captive monster complained non-stop in the back seat, and headed back to put him in a cage.

All in all, it was a good day.

And they'd managed to kill two birds with one stone.

The Chief was sitting behind his desk when they dragged Viktor Vlasik through the door and walked him back to his cell. The loud click of the cell door shutting was music, sweet as a vintage wine or a passage from Vivaldi's Four Seasons played on a Stradivarius violin.

They both turned at the sound of Chief Irwin's voice behind them. "Well, what have we here?"

As they told him their story, the edited version, the Chief blew out a sigh from deep inside his lungs, his wheeze making it sound like a deflating balloon or an untuned bagpipe. "Damn near a miracle," he said, clearing his throat. "Well done." He took a shot from his rescue inhaler and walked back into his office, relieved to have two crimes solved and off his plate. It was one hell of a slam bang beginning but there were still all those broken necks that weren't going to solve it themselves.

And that report of the body out in the desert, which was probably nothing. Nothing at all.

THIRTY-TWO

Thursday morning Trick Delgado and William Washington were assigned to cruising the town, in separate squad cars so as to cover more territory. That was fine with Trick. On his way out he needed to stop by the store to pick up groceries and cat food for his unappreciative mother. It was never easy, being the crap-shoot kid that nature had chosen to be the son of Peggy Delgado. Sometimes he wondered what the god or gods that made those decisions were thinking. And his mother was probably wondering why they chose to have her knocked up by a father who'd abandoned them both shortly after his birth. But they were stuck with each other. He figured they both made the best they could out of a bad situation.

Maybe it was some kind of test.

He was smacked in the face by the smell of cat urine when he entered the house. Dirty dishes stacked high in the sink had an odor all their own. Couldn't she do anything herself? But her acts of martyrdom no longer phased him. He was wise to her and she knew it, but she still wouldn't give up the game. It was her own special dance and she knew every step by heart.

"It's about time," she muttered, standing by the counter as he emptied the bags onto the table. Trick looked down to the floor where the bedraggled cat looked up at him with pleading eyes. The poor cat had been a stray that she took in, which made his situation all the worse. He was an indoor cat who'd never smell fresh air again. He'd become her prisoner with no means of escape.

But Trick knew right where the door was.

"I don't have time for this today, Ma. I've got a full day ahead of me."

And he was out the door before she could say another word.

* * * *

Jim Bullock was assigned the job of driving all the way out to Cabesa Prieta to a deserted spot on the map that Chief Irwin had handed him between bouts of coughing up phlegm. It was to be more like a procession. Jim would be in the lead in his squad car, followed by an ambulance, followed by two city workers with shovels and a small backhoe, should they be needed. Someone had reported finding a body out there and Jim had been given strict orders. If it was nothing but another hundred year old skeleton of some old minor or crosser he was to let it lie, turn around and come back.

But if it was more recent, they were obligated to try and figure out who it was. If it was natural or murder. In that case it was to be dug up and brought back.

The first option was the easy out.

The three vehicles made their way along the hot desert road, slowing to a crawl when the map showed Jim they were nearing their destination. It was difficult telling one part of this area from another. Everything looked the same for mile after boring mile. He finally spotted the area, several feet after an unexplained curve in the long, straight road and pulled over. The other two vehicles pulled up behind him and killed their engines. They all exited their cars and inhaled some hot desert air.

"Sorry you three had to make the drive. It's probably for nothing, but stay here while I check things out. I'll give a yell if I need you."

He walked away, keeping his eyes on the desert floor as he searched for the body. The person who had reported it said it was a bit of a walk from the road but easy to spot. Great day for a hike, Jim thought, with the hot sun beating down on him.

A rock, just large enough to cause trouble, caught the edge of his shoe throwing him off balance. He steadied himself and when he looked down that's when he saw the disturbed earth.

Near the rock a hand jutted out from beneath the desert floor. It was a female hand with a faint hint on its long, broken fingernails of what had once been bright red nail polish. Jim knelt down beside it to take a closer look.

There was something emanating from this poor soul lost between hell and nowhere. An aura of depression surrounded it, thick and strong and dark as the center of some distant universe. A soft, hot breeze caressed the beads of perspiration on his arm and sent chills through him. He'd seen dead bodies before, but something about the forgotten ones always got to him. They were the ones nobody missed. The lost lives that were dispensable, as if their lives as well as their deaths, meant nothing.

Everybody's life meant something.

You've found me. You've finally found me.

For a split second Jim thought he'd heard a voice, but it was only the breeze. Or the sound of the sand beneath the feet of some desert creature seeking a spot of shade.

Take me home.

Jim reached for the boney arm, turning it from side to side. Leathered strips of skin clung to it in places. This body wasn't a hundred years old.

He rose and yelled out to the waiting men, waving his arms and yelling again.

"Shovels or backhoe?" One of them yelled back to him.

"Shovels!"

I want to go home. You'll take me now, won't you? I've been here so long.

The men with the shovels reached Jim, the ambulance driver following behind with a stretcher, just in case.

"Dig around the parameter as widely as possible so we don't stir up the bones. I want this as much intact as possible."

"Sure thing."

The men stood across from each other, leaving a wide gape between them as they kicked their shovels into the ground. They were putting their full weight into it with little to no progress, but they kept at it.

"Damn ground is like trying to dig through concrete," one of them complained, the one smart enough to be wearing a blue bandana across his forehead to catch the sweat and keep it from burning his eyes.

"No shit," said the other one as he intermittently swept a forearm over his wet brow. "Darn near need a chisel to break through this shit."

Jim sat on the ground and rested, listening to the comments and complaints and grunts growing louder as the hole grew deeper and the sun sunk lower. They were making progress but it was going to be a long day. Jim was glad it wasn't his job, all that digging.

By late afternoon the tedious job was complete, the skeleton fully exposed and ready to be gently removed and carried to the waiting stretcher for the long ride back to Agua Verde.

Home.

It was only when Jim rose and stood over the grave that he spotted it.

His heart pounded like a kettle drum beneath his chest and his blood ran cold as he stared at the small object that lay coiled within the twisted bones.

THIRTY-THREE

Daylight was being swallowed by the shadows of pending nightfall as the three vehicles returned to Agua Verde. The ambulance that held the remains headed one way, the truck with the backhoe turned towards the city garage, but Jim's car froze at the stop sign, engine rumbling as he took a deep breath. He had somewhere else to go, and it wasn't home. He hesitated, then turned the wheel in the direction of Trick and Ingrid Delgado's house.

This was the first time it wouldn't be a social call and he wasn't looking forward to it. Not one bit. A day that had started as routine had ended in a nightmare. He didn't know where to start. Trick was his best friend, his oldest friend, but he couldn't let that trump the job he had to do. A lot of questions needed answering because none of them made any sense. He looked at his watch. They should be sitting down to dinner by now, but this was one night that the dessert course would be bitter rather than sweet.

Jim pulled into the driveway and killed the engine. He sat in the car and watched as twilight turned to dark like an ominous blanket attempting to hide long held secrets. Jim's mind lifted the edge of that blanket and looked underneath. He didn't like what he saw. An eternity passed as he worked up the courage, then exited the car and walked up to the front door. He knocked, he rang the bell, he waited. No one answered.

Something wasn't right. None of it was right.

Where was Trick? Where was Ingrid?

He returned to his car, tires squealing as he threw it into reverse and headed toward the home of Peggy Delgado, Trick's mother. Maybe the two of them had gone there. He knew Ingrid avoided visiting with her, but it was worth a shot. He was relieved when he saw Trick's car parked at an awkward angle in her driveway. Like he'd been in a hurry to get there. Was something wrong with her? Maybe a health emergency? He'd met Trick's mother a few times and she did look fragile, until the venom started spewing from her mouth. Playing helpless was part of her game. A sympathy ploy. But Jim didn't have an ounce of pity for the woman. He didn't like her. She was cold and ill-tempered and made no attempt to hide it. A woman who lovingly cuddled her cat yet seemed determined to keep her only son in a world of hurt and confusion. Jim felt for his friend, but respected his support of her no matter how difficult. Peggy Delgado was the queen of mind-games and Trick was her favorite target. Trick was stuck with the mother he got. But a visit with her must have been like strolling through a field of land mines, Trick forever sidestepping his way through them as he manipulated his way through and out the other side.

Once again his knock on the door went unanswered.

The car was there. They had to be inside.

The door was unlocked, so he turned the knob and went inside.

It was quiet.

Too quiet.

Slowly, Trick walked down the hallway, his nose assaulted by the smell of urine and yesterday's garbage. His eyes burned from the fumes as he turned left and into the kitchen. The cat was standing on the kitchen floor, his tongue carefully maneuvering between the shards of broken glass from his food bowl as he licked carefully and patiently at his dinner.

An arm stretched out from behind the kitchen island, still and silent as if reaching out toward the cat. Jim stepped into the room and past the island where the body of Peggy Delgado lay lifeless on the linoleum floor, her eyes like clouded opals, held an expression of surprise. There was no blood.

Her head was tilted at an awkward, unnatural position.

Her neck was broken, he didn't need a coroner to verify that. It didn't take an expert in forensics to see the obvious. Someone had killed her, neat and tidy, unlike her surroundings.

Jim slowly backed his way out of the room and proceeded to sweep his way from room to room, gun in hand. The silence was deafening as he wondered if he'd also find the bodies of Ingrid and Trick lying as lifeless as Peggy's. He steeled himself expecting to find the worst. Each room was eerily empty. And deadly silent. He opened the door to the third bedroom which was lit by a glaring overhead ceiling light. The wallpaper was aged and yellowed, covered in a pattern of cowboys and horses galloping along the sagebrush. It was a child's room. A single bed sat under the window, covered with a dusty blanket. The bookshelf to its left held an array of children's books. There were Albert Payson Terhune dog stories, Jack London adventure tales, a plastic coated book with pages curled up at the corners, the kind of book a child could read in the bathtub or drool his lunch on without damaging it. A well loved and frequently read little book. The shelf also held a scattering of small toys. There were just a few, but they too looked well played with, the brightly painted edges faded with wear from tiny fingers.

Then Jim looked down. Against the wall, beside an open closet door, Trick was sitting on the floor staring up at him.

"Trick?"

"Patrick, Patrick!" he spat out the words, eyes that stabbed like knives stared up at him, with a look he'd never seen before. Antagonistic and angry.

This wasn't Trick he was facing. This wasn't his friend.

"What are you doing here?" the voice growled, more an accusation than a question. "Go away and leave me alone. I've got work to do. Can't you see that?"

"What did you do to your mother?" Jim's voice was a whisper as he holstered his gun, refusing to believe for a second that his friend could be a threat. "What happened to Peggy?"

"That bitch? I gave her what she deserved. I should've done it years ago."

"Why? Why would you do that?"

"Because she was a monster. You don't know what she did to me. Her little boy. She'd beat me in the face because I reminded her of my father. I was too young to fight back when she'd burn me with her cigarettes and laugh at me when I cried. She hated me from the day I was born and I didn't understand why."

"I'm sorry. I had no idea."

"There's some things you don't talk about. Not even to your best friend."

But the man sitting on the floor wasn't the friend Jim knew. He was a total stranger.

"You killed her."

"I had to. You don't hurt little children!"

"Oh Trick…"

"Patrick!" he growled. "Patrick!" He lifted his arms, pressed his hands against his head, pain furrowing his brow as he groaned. "Stop. Why don't they just stop." Jim recognized that look. It was the look Trick got whenever one of his migraines was starting to hit.

He stood above his friend, speechless, not knowing how to help him. He was still trying to grasp the scenario that was unfolding before him, but knowing in his heart that there was no way to help.

There was a shriek that turned into a whimper as his friend rocked back and forth, pressing his hands against his head, trying to force the painful migraine outward and away. A deep sigh exhaled from the man's lungs and he looked up at Jim.

It was Trick's eyes that looked up at him. The friend he treasured.

"Jim?" He looked confused. "What are you doing here?"

"I was looking for you, Trick. I didn't know where to find you."

"Well, damn good thing you did," he said, excitement in his voice. "I told you I was going to solve it. I told you I'd find out who was framing me."

"Trick? Trick, where is Ingrid?"

"Ingrid. I'm not sure. At home I guess." he shook off the question. "Jim," his voice filled with pride. "I did it. I solved it, didn't I?"

"Just like you said you would."

Trick reached over to an old cigar box that sat on the floor next to him, the kind where kids keep their treasures, spilling out its contents. "It was hiding here, in the closet."

Jim looked down at the small items on the floor.

"It's a trophy box. It holds the answers but I don't understand. I don't understand."

Several items were strewn about and Jim recognized a few of them. The necklace with the Asian symbol that Mr. Wong had said was missing from his wife's body. But one in particular stopped him cold. As much as we wanted them to be wrong, his suspicions were right. It was a small, green shamrock earring, identical to the one that he had spotted in the shallow grave earlier that day. It had been Rosy's earring. Rosy. The ex-wife who always wore them with exaggerated pride of her Irish heritage. The ex-wife who had deserted Trick and gone back to the south of Boston to be with family. But she had never gone to Boston. She'd taken a nap under the sands of the desert out by Camino del Diablo.

And somebody had put her there.

Trick was looking at Jim. There were tears in his eyes as he held the gun in his hand. "I don't understand. I don't remember," he said. Then, with pride in his voice, "I solved it, Jim. Didn't I?" He repeated the phrase again, as if seeking Jim's approval.

"Yes, you solved it Trick. You're a good cop."

Trick raised the gun to his temple.

"No, don't! We can take care of this, Trick. We can make it better."

Before Jim could reach him, Trick pulled the trigger.

THIRTY-FOUR

Jim was dazed as he walked out of the house into the black, starless night. He didn't know what to feel, how to sort out the mixture of anger, sadness, total puzzlement and loss. He just stood there, between Trick's car and his own, trying to collect himself enough to report what he had to report.

He was a friend. And he was a cop. A good one. He knew what he was going to have to do and it wasn't going to be easy.

Then he heard something. The sound was faint, but he'd definitely heard it. He listened. It was coming from the trunk of Trick's car. A muffled voice, a weak scratching against metal. He ran over to the car, to the locked trunk and could hear the sounds coming from inside. A female voice. He ran to his car and removed a crowbar from his own trunk and returned, pushing crowbar against metal with all his force. It felt like forever before he was finally able to pop the trunk open.

It was Ingrid. She was safe. She was curled up inside, sweaty and weak and gasping for breath. He reached in and pulled her out, holding her tightly against him. She appeared unharmed, but if he hadn't heard her she would have suffocated. She would have been the last victim, rather than Trick himself.

"Where's Trick?" she asked when she finally found her voice. "Is he okay? What's happening?"

He replayed it for her, as gently as he could. There was nothing gentle about death. There was no way to sugar coat it and make it sound like less than it was.

"Oh, Jim," she said, choking back the tears. "I'd been turning a blind eye. I'd been living in denial for so long because I love him. I loved him so much. But the clues were there all along. I just didn't want to see them."

"I don't understand any of it."

"How could I not have seen it? There was the Trick we both loved and he was a good man. Truly he was. But sometimes," she paused. "Sometimes he was, well," she searched for the right words. "Sometimes he was different. It was like somebody flipped a switch. No wonder he never talked about his time with Special Forces. He couldn't remember half of it,

Jim. The headaches, it was always after the headaches. He'd become more aggressive, angry, even more passionate in his love-making. He just wasn't Trick anymore. He was someone else."

Jim stood silently and listened.

"I've spent years dealing with abused kids in my job. Some psychologist I turned out to be! It's rare Jim, but sometimes child abuse can do things to a person. And Peggy was definitely an abuser. My God, what that poor man went through as a child. On rare occasion the personality splits. A second personality emerges. One that can handle the abuse. One that deals with it. During those times the dominant, main personality blacks out and the other takes over. Neither one is aware of the others existence. Those were the times Trick got confused, the times when there were gaps in his memory that he couldn't explain. Poor Trick."

"I think I saw them both tonight," said Jim. "The one that said 'you don't hurt little children', that one insisted his name was Patrick."

She paused. "Patrick had sensed that I was on to him. That's how I ended up in the trunk of the car. Trick would never hurt me, but Patrick needed to get rid of me."

Then it all clicked in Jim's head. It all fell into place. Mrs. Wong wasn't nice to her little son Winston. Tina Weston, the addict, had abused and neglected her son. The boyfriend, Joey Palermo, had done nothing to help. He hadn't hanged himself in his cell. He'd had help. Maybe Rosy had figured him out too, or maybe he just didn't want her to leave him. Or? It didn't really matter any more. She was dead and gone. But Peggy Delgado was the worst of all. All of them dead. All of them with broken necks, an efficient and quick maneuver Trick, no, Patrick would have learned during his military training. And what about Benjamin Bordain? He was no child abuser and his death had been ruled an accident. Jim thought for a minute. Could it have been Trick who was leaving Wong's as Benji, Snorkel and Whitey the Werewolf were entering the store? Was he afraid that Benji could recognize him?

It all made sense now.

Every bit of it.

EPILOGUE

THREE MONTHS LATER

The first chill of impending autumn came in on a soft breeze, like the flutter of moth wings.

The heat of summer was finally behind them, like a predator slinking silently away. The friends sat on the back porch sipping their beers and looking up at the night sky. The moon was full, rising up toward the highest fronds of the palm tree. Stars filled the sky, filling the world beneath with wonder and promise. A promise of better days to come. Ingrid rose and headed into the house, then returned with three cold beers to replenish their supply. They were letting go of the past and moving forward together. They were enjoying the buzz and savoring the moment. Big Jim Bullock was there. And William Washington sat next to him, one hand resting against Jim's arm. Through all the tragedy the three had bonded and formed a strong friendship. Ingrid had always liked Jim, but since he'd rescued her from the trunk of Trick's car he'd become even more than that. They still missed Trick and always would. But life went on.

It always did.

It had to.

Back at the station Chief Irwin was breaking in two more rookies. And the desks were filling with new crimes to solve. Petty crimes, just how the cops of Agua Verde liked it. On the back porch Jim looked up at the stars, each one reminding him of Paco, the enthusiastic little man who had stolen his heart and brought so much color to his life. It was a chapter of his life he'd always hold close to his heart. The pain, the joy, all of it.

He looked over at William Washington and knew he would be part of his future.

The three of them raised their beer bottles, clinking them against each other.

"Here's to friendship," said Ingrid. "And a brighter tomorrow."

ABOUT THE AUTHOR

Lonni Lees is a multiple award-winning writer of fiction, nonfiction, and poetry. Her stories have appeared in *Hardboiled* magazine, *Yellow Mama, A Shot of Ink, Shotgun Honey, Black Petals, Einstein's Pocket Watch, All Due Respect*, and in the anthologies *Deadly Dames, More Whodunits, Felons, Flames and Ambulance Rides*, and *Battling Boxing Stories*. Her short fiction can be found her collection, *Crawlspace*.

Broken is her fourth published novel. Her first novel, *Deranged*, won the PSWA award for best published novel. Her second novel, *The Mosaic Murder*, was followed with a sequel, *The Corpse in the Cactus*, which won First Place and was published in the US and UK. She has won several other awards for her short stories.

She received both art and a non-fiction Creative Writing Award from NLAPW, California South branch, an organization of women writers, artists and composers, where she also served as President from 1982 to 1984 . A current member of Sisters in Crime, PSWA, and Arizona Mystery Writers (where she was the first writer to win two consecutive awards in their annual short story contest).

Lonni was twice selected as Writer in Residence at Hedgebrook, a writer's retreat on Whidbey Island. After living in four states and visiting many countries, she's settled in Tucson. She fills her spare time showing her art at WomanKraft Gallery, reminiscing on all her travel adventures, illustrating stories for on-line magazines, and dreaming up new tales to tell.

www.ingramcontent.com/pod-product-compliance
Lightning Source LLC
Chambersburg PA
CBHW020143180626
46810CB00004B/1710
* 9 7 8 1 4 7 9 4 5 0 9 1 6 *